THAT'S WHEN I KISSED HER . . .

Which is when all the nosy little kids popped their heads out of the room and watched.

"Ooooooooooooooooooooooooooooooooooh!" they said.

I stopped kissing for a second, looked at them, and pointed. "Some day you'll understand!" I said.

Not Just Another Pretty Face

PETER FILICHIA

NOT JUST ANOTHER PRETTY FACE is an original publication of Avon Books. This work has never before appeared in book form.

AVON BOOKS
A division of
The Hearst Corporation
105 Madison Avenue
New York, New York 10016

Published by arrangement with the author
Library of Congress Catalog Card Number: 87-91626
ISBN: 0-380-75244-1
RL: 5.4

First Avon Flare Printing: January 1988

Printed in the U.S.A.

K-R 10 9 8 7 6 5 4 3

The Author Would Like To Thank:
JOHN HARRISON
And
LINDA KONNER
Two People With Great Inner Beauty

DALLINEWS

The Newspaper of Dallin High School
Ardmore, Massachusetts

LARAH LAVERY WINS REGIONAL 'OUTSTANDING YOUNG WOMAN' CONTEST

by Bill Richards

SATURDAY, FEBRUARY 8TH—At a contest held Saturday night at O'Gorman Hall, Larah Lavery, a senior at Dallin High School, was selected from a total of 21 Ardmore girls as the candidate who will represent the town in the upcoming Miss Outstanding Young Woman Contest.

Next month, Larah will compete with 64 girls from other Massachusetts towns for the title of "Massachusetts's Most Outstanding Young Woman." That competition will be held on March 31st in John Hancock Hall in Boston.

For the entertainment portion of the contest, Larah read Emma Lazarus's stirring sonnet, "The New Colossus."

Larah is 5′9″ tall, has blonde hair and hazel eyes. She'll be 18 years old this November 8th. She lives at 10 Cutting Lane, in the Morningside section of town.

A member of the Drama Club, Larah appeared as a Lady-in-Waiting in last year's production of *Once Upon a Mattress*.

The Miss Outstanding Young Woman Contest began in 1967, but this is the first time that a girl from Dallin has gotten this far. Let's hope that Larah will be the first to win the top prize. Good luck, Larah!

1

"And," I said, "I hope that's the last 'Outstanding' Larah Lavery story."

Mike spun around from the computer, Luke looked up from Robin Ziegler's new poem, and Doug swiveled around in his chair.

"Hey," Luke said, getting real excited, straddling his legs around the chair legs and leaning his chest against where your back's supposed to go. "Larah Lavery's pretty outstanding when she dances, I'll tell you that." He drummed his hands against the back of the chair. "Can she move it! Sometimes when I watch her out there on the floor, the way she moves—you know what I mean?"

"I know what you mean," I droned.

"I mean," Luke went on, "she's out there dancin', and then she leans over to her left, leaning over, leaning over. . . ." Luke jumped out of the chair. "*Va-boom!* Half the time I swear she's gonna tip over. I'm almost yellin', 'Watch out, honey, don't tip over and hurt yourself!' But no, just when I think she's going to fall on the floor, she pulls herself up—I don't know how she does it, but she does it—and then she starts dancin' and leaning over to her right, leaning over, leaning over. . . ."

Doug, who sometimes looks like one of those old-fashioned accountant types that wear little green eyeshades to protect their eyes, wanted to let Luke know he didn't think Larah was too outstanding, either. "So she can dance," he said dryly.

Luke, though, didn't hear anything in Doug's voice. 'Wow!" he yelled, plopping back into his chair. "I loved it this winter—when she wore those long, long leg warmers on those long, long legs. Though," he added, "I'm really looking forward to spring, a real hot spring, I hope, when she wears hardly anything. Oh," he suddenly remembered, "and that *hair!*"

And that hair. Yeah, that made us all quiet, as we thought about that long, straight, straw-colored hair that flows down her back . . . floats on top of it, really . . . and is cut in a perfect straight line, straight across, right at her waist. Problem is, that hair also reminds me of my old girlfriend April's, a girl who'll someday probably grow up to sell top secrets to the enemy, since she's so good at betraying people. Yeah, April . . . who was probably right then and there letting her Greek god of a boyfriend handle that beautiful hair, and everything else. . . .

No. I promised myself I wouldn't think about her, and I wouldn't.

"Larah's hair," Luke went on, "always looks so great, I'm sure she washes it and does whatever girls do with their hair four times a day."

"You've got to give credit where credit is due," I said, repeating the line Ms. Naiman, our adviser, says a lot. "She's got the looks, I'll give her that—"

Luke spread the arms that brought a lot of grief to enemy wide receivers last season. "I'll give her more than that. I'll give her everything I got. When it comes to looks, she's as 'outstanding' as anyone you see—on videos, in magazines, the movies, on cable. Or should I just say that she's the most outstanding-looking girl in *life?*''

Doug smiled. ''You said magazines.''

It took us a second to get the joke (it usually does anytime Doug makes one of his jokes) but when we finally realized that he meant *Life*'s a magazine, too, we all started groaning the way everybody does when they hear a pun—even though, to tell the truth, we all thought it was a pretty good one. But, after all, even after terrific puns everyone's expected to groan.

''Anyway,'' I said, ''there are a few reasons why Larah isn't outstanding.''

Luke gave me a who-you-kidding look. ''You're just mad she wouldn't drop that senior from Boston College for you.'' Then he decided to make some sort of joke. ''Or did you get something off her for putting her on the front page?''

''Right,'' I said, scowling. ''You made a big mistake when you decided to cover intramural basketball instead of the pageant.''

Mike was scowling, too. Our editor in chief sometimes looks like Alfred E. Neuman of *Mad* magazine fame, but when he's serious, he looks more like the guy on *Nightline*, Ted Koppel. ''As if Larah didn't know she was going to make our front page.''

''Yeah,'' Doug agreed. ''We need her more than she needs us.''

I had to agree with that. ''At least she's a story the kids are interested in.''

''*Dallin May Buy Warehouse to Use for Classrooms,*'' Mike muttered, quoting last month's headline, the most boring one we ever ran.

''And if you think that was bad,'' Luke said, ''wait till you see Robin's new poem.''

"What's this one about?"

"How the Statue of Liberty's lips look like Elvis Presley's."

"They do in a way," I said, making them all look at me like I was crazy, too.

Mike scowled again. "But what can we do? Print the bad stuff we know about Larah? No newspaper that's any good prints rumors, and Ms. Naiman wouldn't let us do it, anyway."

"No," Doug agreed, lifting his eyebrows high, smiling away, "but wouldn't it be great if we could run an issue where we told the whole truth about Larah?"

"Hah!" I laughed. "All the news that isn't fit to print."

"I can see the headline now," Doug said, waving his hand in front of him. *"Larah Writes Down Wrong Number."*

All of us started laughing, except for Luke, who just transferred to Dallin this year. "Luke," Mike asked. "D'ja ever hear the story about the time Larah baby-sat for Jeff Lonergan's parents?"

Luke shook his head no.

Doug jumped into telling the story, too. "Jeff's got a baby sister, so one night his parents needed someone to baby-sit her, and, I don't know how, somehow they got Larah—"

"—so she baby-sits," Mike took over. "And when Jeff gets home that night, he walks in and sees his mother and father laughing like crazy."

"Larah had just left," I explained, "and they're laughing because of what they'd just read on the message pad next to the telephone."

"Someone had called up."

"And Larah took down a message."

"And it said . . ."

We all said it together: " 'A wrong number called.' "

Now I know I have a loud laugh, but Luke's is—well, a few weeks ago I went with him to the movies, and half the audience was turning around to see who was laughing like that, while the other half must have been wondering how the hyena got in the theater. And right then, when he heard Larah thought even a wrong number was something a sitter should write down, he laughed for a solid minute before he started to cough like crazy and we had to do some serious back thumping. Then, after he recovered, he said, "Nawwwwwwww! She didn't do that!"

But we all kept nodding our heads. "Lonergan still carries around the message-pad piece of paper in his wallet."

"And the handwriting checked out. We compared it with her subscription form."

"Little circles over the *i*'s."

"She ended the sentence with a heart instead of a period, just like she did on the abbreviation *St.*"

"Well, all right," Luke said, "*maybe* someone could be that stupid. I can kinda see my brother doing that."

"What else would we print in our 'Truth about Larah' issue?" Doug asked, wanting to continue the fantasy, and then answering his own question. "I'd also write a first-person story on 'What It's Like to Be Behind Larah in a Revolving Door.' Ever done it? Once she gets in her little section, she doesn't push to help the thing move. She just walks along, hands at her side, expecting you and the guy in front to do the pushing for her. Watch her sometime."

"The lead for my Larah story," Mike said, "would

be, 'Larah Lavery is not the most sympathetic kid in the world.' "

Boy, could I relate to that. . . .

"Last winter," he went on, "when Debbie MacLean got in that accident, I was next to Larah in line in the caf, telling her how it was looking real bad for Debbie. All the while I'm talking, Larah's looking over the food, getting a cup of coffee, nodding her head, and not saying anything. I didn't think she was listening, but I figured, well, maybe she is. But then, when I got to the worst part, she just said, 'Do you see any Sweet 'n Low around? I can't believe they're out of Sweet 'n Low.' "

Luke had to laugh a little at that, too. I didn't, because it reminded me of the terrible thing I'd seen Larah do a month before—so terrible I hadn't even felt like telling anyone about it. And even though this seemed to be the perfect time and place to tell the story, I didn't want to do it now.

"Bill," Mike asked me, "what picture would we run in our special 'Truth about Larah' issue?"

I knew what story he wanted me to tell. Okay—that one I'd do.

"Last year," I began, "we needed a picture of Larah to run with a cheerleading story, so I asked her for one. *One*. She came in here with something that looked like a suitcase full of pictures. For a half hour, we went through every picture she had. 'Do you like this one?' 'What do think of this?' 'I don't know if I like this.' 'Would you like a profile instead of one that shows my whole face?' And after a half hour of that, what did she decide? That *none* of the pictures was any good, and she'd have to have a new one taken just for us."

"Okay," Luke said, sounding bored, "so she worries about the way she looks, and she doesn't push a door, and she takes down one message too many. But so what? Even someone outstanding is still going to be only human."

There was a silence, because nobody had another story to tell. Except me. And I wasn't going to let Luke think that Larah hadn't done anything so wrong.

So I had to say, "She's done something worse than that."

Luke looked at me and so did the other guys. I guess I wanted to tell my story after all.

"A month ago, I was covering cheerleaders' tryouts—"

"You get all the luck."

"—in that famous warehouse Dallin was thinking of buying for classrooms. Anyway," I breathed, "there we all were, up on the eighth floor, where all the girls were doing their splits and shakes, or whatever they're called, all of them trying to get a place on the cheerleading team Larah's captain of. One girl—Elaine Steiner, just a sophomore, you might not know her—really wanted to make the team. She's pretty, and she was knocking herself out like crazy, but to be honest about it, even I could see she wasn't as good as everyone else was, and what do I know about cheerleading? Anyway, at the end of the tryouts, Ms. Finberg had to tell the kid she hadn't made the cut.

"All right. Little while later I went to the men's room, and when I came out, the only kids left in the place are Elaine and Larah. Elaine had her back to the elevator door, waiting for it to come up to the eighth floor, and I could hear her trying to be brave about what had happened, complimenting Larah on how good she was, and how she wished she could be like her. Then—with her back still to the door now—

Elaine heard the 'ping' and heard the elevator doors open up. She started to take a step backwards into it while she was still talking to Larah. And then," I said, letting disgust show in my voice, "Larah said, 'Watch out, Elaine! You're going to fall! The elevator's not there!' "

They were as stunned as I'd been. "*What?*"

"Are you kidding?"

"Naw!"

"Of course the elevator *was* there. But the look on Elaine's face was horrible. She really believed it wasn't there, and that she was going to fall the whole eight flights. She tried to stop stepping backwards and pull herself forward, and of course she couldn't. She wound up falling backwards, where of course the elevator car was all along. Then the door closed. And then Larah laughed, like it was some kind of really great joke."

"God," Luke said softly. "What a witch."

Mike agreed. "Wish the contest judges knew *that* Larah Lavery."

"Be real," Doug said, his long face looking even longer than usual. "We can all figure out what the judges liked. All those contests are alike."

Luke pointed a you've-got-that-right finger, and now everybody was nodding heads and agreeing.

"Yup," Mike said. "They saw her looks, she turned on the charm, changed her whole personality, and fooled the judges."

"Well," Doug said, half-seriously, "when Ms. Naiman gets out of the hospital, let's see if she'll let us write a 'Truth about Larah' issue."

"Yeah, right."

"How is she anyway?" Luke wanted to know.

"Ms. Naiman? No new news."

"It'll still be a few weeks."

"But the doctors say she's really coming along for a woman who had such a serious operation."

Then came one of those big pauses when nobody had anything else to say, so I just looked at my watch.

"I've got to get to work. Anybody need a ride?"

Luke held up his copy and pointed it toward Mike. "Gotta see what the boss thinks of this."

"Okay, then. See you tomorrow."

"Before school," Mike said, cocking his head. "Karen's called a meeting."

"I'll be there," I said, remembering that Karen, our financial manager, had been hitting us up for some new ideas to sell more papers. I hadn't thought of anything yet, but one thing was for sure: We couldn't afford to run any more headlines like *Dallin May Buy Warehouse to Use for Classrooms*. That issue didn't sell beans.

2

I left ''home plate'' and started walking to The On-Deck Circle to get a quick snack before going to work.

It was Kevin Feeley, editor of the paper when I was a freshman, who realized that the layout of Dallin was a lot like a baseball diamond, because the school's four buildings sit where the four bases do in a ballpark. The Administration Building is where home plate'd be, first base is the Arts and Science Building; the Mathematics Building is second, and O'Gorman Hall is third.

After Kevin came up with that, everyone got into it—the gazebo in the middle of the campus became known as the pitcher's mound, and the little grocery store tucked away right off campus eventually changed its name from Sam's to The On-Deck Circle.

When I was just about to go into The Circle, I looked at my watch and decided that no, why have a Drake's cake or a couple of Hostess Sno Balls when I still had time to get a doughnut from the best doughnut-maker of all?

Yes—I'd have time for a honeydip at Eddie's.

If my car felt like starting, that is. The '74 Mustang had been ornery lately, but what do you want for $250?

As I took the long walk up Hemlock Street, where a lot of us kids park (because they only let teachers park in the school parking lot), I thought a little more about Larah. Bad as the elevator incident was, I had to wonder if all of us were saying those things against her because we were jealous. Ordinary-looking people are sometimes a little jealous of great-looking people. Sometimes they're even plenty jealous.

And I'm just an ordinary-looking guy . . . with ordinary brown eyes, ordinary brown hair . . . and an ordinary face (yes, cheeks that are a little chubbier than ordinary and redden up like crazy in the winter, but other than that, I'm pretty ordinary-looking).

Sure, I could look a lot worse, with a face that'd make people scream in horror, throw down their groceries, and run the other way. Still, it would've been more fun to be a little more than just ordinary . . . more than just five ordinary feet and nine ordinary inches tall—the same height as Larah, by the way, which made her model-tall, and put me in the lower-middle percentage of the senior guys. . . .

But as I got in my car, pressed the gas pedal, and hoped for the best, I had to wonder about one thing, something I didn't tell any of the guys: If Larah hadn't lately become friends with April, ever since they joined that stupid high school sorority, would I be this much against her?

Ga-chorfa, gachorfa, gachorfa, said my ignition when I turned it. *Gachorfa, gachorfa, gachorfa.*

Okay, I thought, don't panic. I waited a sec, pressed the gas pedal again, waited again—maybe not as long as I should have, but I couldn't stand the suspense.

Gachorfa, gachorfa, gachorfa-va-ROOOOM.

Whew.

I started driving. It was 3:26 now, getting late, but if a space was open on the lot behind Eddie's, I'd have enough time to stop by and still be at the hotel by 4:00.

I hoped that Eddie had just made up a new batch of honeydips. Sure, eight-hour-old Eddie's Donuts are still better than anybody else's, but the ones that come right out of the oven are so light and crumbly they almost should be marked "Fragile."

Just like there are cult movies and cult groups, Eddie's is a cult doughnut shop. A lot of people in Ardmore go to the mall or to one of the famous doughnut shops they see advertised on TV, but there's a small, steady group of us who don't care that Eddie's isn't the most modern place in the world, or that he doesn't have 204 varieties to choose from. What Eddie does give us is great doughnuts, so we make sure we give him enough business so he can get by.

We've gotten to be friends, Eddie and I. In fact, he's the first real adult friend I've ever had. Dad's a great guy, and so's my Uncle Bob, but relatives don't count—they *have* to like you. Mr. Russo, my old soccer coach, and Mr. Creelman, my favorite teacher, are both great, too, but they're not friends the way Eddie is to me. I know he'd like me, even if I didn't buy doughnuts from him.

So two years ago when I started going in there, I was saying, "Excuse me, may I have a cup of coffee and a honeydip?" Last year it went to, "Hey, Ed, coffee and one of the honeys," and now we were at, "Ed! How ya doing? Can you believe they blew a three-goal lead last night?" all while he's automatically putting coffee and a honeydip in front of me.

For a while, though, I'd also been asking, "Hey, Ed—how are you feeling?" Ed has cataracts, and though he doesn't complain about it, I'm getting the impression just from watching him that it's getting worse. It was one of the reasons April didn't like going in there; she wasn't too good being around people who had a physical problem or two. And she also liked Dunkin' Donuts' pretty pink-and-white walls or Mr. Donut's red-and-blue ones. As for the rest of us, we know Ed's in no mood or condition to paint, so we don't let those not-so-bright-green walls bother us. But April . . .

I knew I'd promised myself I wasn't going to think about her, but I just couldn't stop. I had to wonder once again what would have happened if I'd never gone to the Alumni Homecoming last June. Trouble is, every time I thought that way, it wasn't long before I'd have to admit that I had after all been looking forward to the stupid party for a week.

I wanted to fall in love at that party. And as I got ready, luck seemed to be with me: I looked good that night. I'm not trying to brag, but I have to admit it—I looked as good as I get. Friends of mine sometimes say I look "a little" like Michael J. Fox, but I don't think it's true, because nobody who isn't my friend has ever said it.

But I still looked good, and so I actually made it up the gym stairs before I started to worry about finding the right girl for me. (Usually I start panicking right after I've parked the car.) Sure, the thought of being checked out by a bunch of girls was kind of scary, and the thought that they might not even bother to keep looking once they saw me was even worse. And as good as I looked, I still wasn't any match for the kids who look a lot more like Michael J. Fox than I do.

And besides, my car's a piece of junk, which doesn't help at all in getting a girl or keeping her interested in you.

I was glad to see that Mike and Doug were already at the party. We talked a lot about what we were going to do with *Dallinews* next year, what with the seniors gone and now us, the new seniors, in charge. But if I'm going to be honest about it, I have to admit that all during talk like "Why can't we think up an idea for at least one interesting new column?" I was only half-listening. What we were really doing was checking out every great-looking girl in the place.

So after we'd discussed everything for a while (or, as they say on the news every night, *allegedly* discussed), I decided we should face the facts:

"We're not listening to each other, are we?"

"I'm listening," Doug said.

"The way you do when you're doing homework with the TV on."

"I can pay attention to both."

"Let's admit it," I said. "All through this whole conversation one eye has been traveling half out of the socket trying to check out if that good-looking smiling blonde over there is smiling because she likes one of us or because she's heard a good joke."

"It was a good joke," Mike said, known for his great powers of eavesdropping.

"So what do you suggest?" Doug asked.

I shrugged. "All I mean is I don't just want to stand around and . . ."

I stopped talking because I saw a girl smile in my direction . . . or Mike's direction . . . or Doug's direction. (I couldn't be sure.) Actually, she turned out to be looking at a guy behind us who looked too old to be here.

"That guy's got to be at least 22."

"Why did they have to tell the school's graduates about this? Yeah, I know it was an Alumni Homecoming—"

"—but still . . ."

"Come on," Mike said, "it's hot in here. Let's go outside and talk."

"No," I said. "You know what we're doing wrong? We're sticking together. A girl doesn't have the guts to come up to a whole group of guys."

I looked at Mike. He looked at me. We nodded our heads once, looked at Doug, and waited for him to nod back. Finally he did.

"I'll go east," I said.

"I'll go west," Mike decided.

"I'll stay here," Doug said.

Even so, for a split second nobody moved. Then we looked at each other like we were about to embark on some sort of life-or-death mission, as I went to the right, Mike went to the left, and, for all I know, Doug kept standing where we left him for the rest of the night. To tell the truth, when I started walking, I didn't even know where I was going. I just walked around for a few minutes, pretending I was interested in the decorations. Except who was I fooling? How interesting is crepe paper, no matter how many colors there are?

So I figured at least if I went to the bar and got an Orange Crush it might look like I was doing something. I also figured I'd kill some time standing around waiting for Mrs. Kochie to get to me—except she's so efficient she waited on me right away.

"Yes, Bill?"

A guy who looked 23 (okay, 20) had just gotten to the bar and hadn't really noticed I was there first (great for my ego). "Um, you first," I said, figuring it'd give me another minute to look around, kill time, maybe catch some girl's eye—which I couldn't.

"Okay, Bill! Your turn!"

"Thanks, Mrs. Kochie. Um, Orange Crush."

Wouldn't you know she had one handy, palmed it over real fast, and went right on to the next customer—leaving me to do nothing but get away from there so all the guys who looked 24 could get what they wanted.

Don't ask me why, but I decided to go into the home ec room, which they'd set up as a kitchen. And to this day I still have the picture in my head. There was this terrific-looking girl with beautiful long hair carrying a bowl of Fritos. (All right, I know it's not the most romantic image in the world, but it's what she was doing—carrying Fritos.)

She was wearing a bright yellow dress with classy high-heeled shoes to match. For earrings, she just wore plain little gold rings that made her look elegant. So did the little gold cross on the gold chain around her neck. And, of course, there was that long, straw-blonde hair flowing right down to her waist, cut in a perfect straight line, in a real elegant way.

And elegant is the word I want. Whoever this girl was, she was smart about her makeup, too. I noticed the girls she seemed to be talking to most—girls I got to know a lot of stuff about over the summer, Lorrie, Elizabeth, Gittel—were the types who wouldn't wear lots of makeup, either. You'd have to look at all these girls for a while before you even realized they had any on.

But I was just looking at this one girl, who was, of

course, April. By the time she smiled at me, I was already in love, and for a change wasn't even afraid to go up and talk to her.

"Hi."

She said it better, "*Hi,*" with a sound in her voice that made me know she was really interested.

No matter what's happened to us since, I'll always swear that when April saw me, she was, like the song goes, hit by a bolt of love. I can still hear that I'm interested "*Hi.*"

I don't dance much, but that night I sure felt like being on the floor all night, especially for the slow dances, which we did slower and slower the later it got. By the end of the night we were really just holding each other while songs played behind us.

I drove her home, and we were parked in front of her house for a nice, long time, as we talked about the kids we knew, the teachers we liked, the ones we thought were crazy. Okay, she didn't know anything about sports, which would have been nice, but I thought it was kind of cute when she mentioned she went to a baseball game last year and the Red Sox won by ten *points*.

Then we started kissing, and kept kissing for a wonderfully long time. I wasn't even worried that her father might come out to find out what we were doing out in front of his house for all that time. What we were doing was the absolutely right thing to do.

When I finally got home and into bed, I was the happiest guy in the world: I'd finally found out there was such a thing as love at first sight. Used to be I'd come home from a dance feeling sorry for myself because I hadn't found anyone, and would it ever happen? But not that night—I sure didn't feel sorry for myself then! Like the team that wins the Super

Bowl, like the Beatles fan who finally finds the rare "Butcher" cover, I'd gotten what I'd wanted.

Three days later, on our first real date, we each said, "I love you." I did something I wouldn't have thought would have been as easy to do as it was: I gave her my brand-new class ring. I didn't care that I'd had it for only about two weeks, didn't care if it cost me $146, didn't care at all, I wanted her to have it. And I knew she'd say yes. Everything was going great!

To make things even better, I was able to get a summer job as a bellman at the Quality Court, and April got one as a waitress at Lizzie's. What was great about that was that because both places stay open 24 hours—and because we were the rookies on the staff—we had to work Saturdays and Sundays. So what? All it meant was that we had Mondays and Tuesdays off together.

We made the most of them. We went to Hampton Beach almost every day off and developed major-league tans. We learned to water-ski, boogie-board, and bodysurf. Then at night we'd walk around holding hands at Hampton's little amusement park. Probably the only time we didn't hold them was when we ate cotton candy or played the old-fashioned pinball machines. I didn't even like cotton candy until I met April, and liked video games better than April's favorite pinballs, but I liked everything that summer—especially when we'd find a moment when everybody was into their own thing and wasn't noticing us, when we'd kiss.

But the best nights of all were when we'd go for dinner at "my" hotel, because everyone knew me, of course, and treated me like I was President and April was First Lady. I felt so great holding her hand as I walked in. Pretty soon everyone got to know *us*. "Bill and April," Mr. Meyers'd say real excited, "good to see you!" as we came in; "Bill and April," said Dolores the hostess on our way out, "you both look so cute."

And then there were the times we'd drive over to Maine, to Ongonquit. Saying a town is "charming" sounds kind of phony, but I don't know what else to call a town that has little gingerbread-house-like cottages surrounded by pretty white picket fences, and saltwater taffy stores, too. We'd walk in and out of little art galleries until the owners' faces made it clear we'd been in there long enough. Once, though, I did buy something: the watercolor April noticed the last time we'd been in there. When she said she liked it a second time, I pulled out the tens and fives from my just-cashed paycheck and bought it. I don't resent spending the money on her—it's what I felt at the time—but now I wonder if she said she liked it just because she wanted to sound like she liked something.

Still, I thought everything was going great—so great I didn't even pay that much attention to the great summer the Red Sox were having and never even asked Mom about the week in the summer I always spend with my father in New York.

Now my father's a really great guy, and he thinks I'm great, too, so we really have phenomenal times together. Mike and Doug are always telling me if Dad and I lived together, we'd be like them and their fathers, not thinking the other's so terrific. Maybe. Dad's kind of neat, I'm kind of messy, and for one week he can stand the clothes, notebooks, and souvenirs all over the place—but if we lived together year-round, I'm pretty sure he'd get on me for being a pig like Mom always does. He'd probably also hassle me too the way she does when I play my Tom Petty and the Heartbreakers albums first thing in the morning, and if I had to hear Montserrat Caballe (and they say rock musicians have funny names) or watch Dad eat one more square of tofu . . .

But I also like going to Dad's because of the phenomenal city New York is. Even though I'm not as hot on video games anymore, it's still nice to have arcades all around you whenever you need them. There's always one terrific musical and play on Broadway, and Dad takes me to both of them. Plenty of movies too in New York that never seem to come to Boston—like a fabulous French one directed by a guy named Philippe DeBroca (whose hand I'd like to shake) called *Give Her the Moon* that Dad and I always try to get to if it's at the Regency, Bleecker St. Cinema, or the Thalia. The Knicks and the Rangers are practically walking distance from Dad's apartment, and the Mets and Yankees are just a subway ride away. The Giants, Jets, Nets, and Devils are right across the river, and even the Islanders aren't hard to get to. What's also great is that all of these teams have real big rivalries with the Boston teams I know and love, so we've seen some amazingly hard-fought games together.

After we come back to his place from whatever we've been doing, there's sometimes a late West Coast game on TV, which we sit and watch, but with the sound off. That way we can keep an eye on what's happening and talk at the same time. Over the years, that's meant such conversations as "How come I'm so short?" (third grade) to "How can I keep from killing my Spanish teacher?" (last year).

And late at night's also when I remember how great it is to be in a city where if you want an Orange

Crush and a slice of pizza at four in the morning, there are a hundred places you can go—places where you might even see Woody Allen or Julian Lennon, which we have.

Okay, have I made myself clear? I love New York. But during that summer with April, I would've rather stayed home around boring old Ardmore, where if you want a can of Orange Crush after eleven o'clock, you'd better hope that Lenny at the Citgo station forgot to take the cans out of the machine. I considered telling Dad I didn't want to come, but I couldn't. I knew it would have hurt him a lot. But I didn't want to leave April any sooner than I had to, either.

Then one day at work it hit me that I'd have to go to New York, but I could at least postpone it until August, even the end of August. Lizzie's Restaurant doesn't let waitresses take personal calls, so I wouldn't be able to tell April I postponed until I picked her up that night.

When I did, she was out in front talking to a guy. Even in the dim moonlight I could tell he looked like a Greek god, more than a Greek god. If they had this guy around in the time of the Greek gods, we'd probably all still be working for Greece today.

Okay . . . she was talking and she was smiling . . . but that didn't mean I had to get nervous. After all, she wasn't doing anything with the guy. He was at least in his twenties, too, so I figured he was much too old for a girl who was just going to be a junior. Besides, she was wearing my ring and promised she wouldn't go out with anybody else, and she loved me, she'd said it. I didn't have to worry.

But I worried.

When she got in the car, I didn't even mention the

guy. "I'm putting off going to see my father till the end of August!"

"How come?"

How come?!?! I expected, "Oh! Wow!! Great!!!" But I didn't tell her that, I just said, "So we can have more time together."

"Oh!"

Hmmm.

Another bad sign that Sunday, when we went to my cousin's wedding. April and I were sitting at the table when all of a sudden April said to me, "Food's not too good, and there's not much of it, is there?" Thank God Mom was talking to Aunt Sally and didn't hear her. Sure, I'll admit she was right on both counts, but if I was the guest at something like this, I wouldn't have brought it up to the guy who brought me. I couldn't help thinking, "Maybe she isn't everything I thought she was."

I didn't know what I felt a few nights later when I went to pick her up and she was out talking to the Greek god again. This time I couldn't not ask her about him; that'd make me look weak. If we were going together, I had the right to ask a question like that.

"Oh, Jim? He's just someone who works in the kitchen."

I wanted to say, "Why didn't you introduce me to him?" but she didn't make him sound important. And I bought that, because I wanted to believe it was true.

I never saw him again when I went to pick her up. Of course I thought that she was seeing him everywhere else around the restaurant, but I didn't have the guts to ever ask her about him. Still, I knew something had changed.

For the next few weeks the days at Hampton and the trips to Ongonquit didn't seem the same anymore. So I suggested new beaches, that we try real surfing, even that we play miniature golf as a joke, *anything* that might make life seem exciting again. When it was time for me to leave to visit my father, I half-wanted to go so I could talk all this over with him—and half-wanted to stay, because I was afraid of what would happen if I left.

A few days before I left, I picked her up and told her this news:

"You know the Brattle Theater, where they show a different two movies every day, old movies?"

"Yeah?"

"I just read in the paper *Give Her the Moon*'s going to be there."

"Oh. That's good."

"Yeah. Only thing is, though, wouldn't you know the only night it's going to be there is when I'm going to be in New York?"

"Ohh," she said, trying, I think, to sound sad.

"Definitely go, though," I said. "You'll really like it."

"Sure," she said, sounding—how? Was she really up for seeing the picture, or just acting excited because it was easier?

Yes, I'd have to talk to Dad.

As soon as we got to the Callahan Tunnel, Mom and I both noticed the airport seemed a lot less crowded than usual.

"It is kind of foggy," I said.

And sure enough, the fog was the reason why: it had come in and grounded all the planes—including mine.

Mom reminded me I could take Amtrak out. All I could think about was what it'd be like when I got hungry, standing in line with four hundred other people in the Club Car—only to get a coffee and Danish pastry I'd have to pay for. Compare that to having a flight attendant serve me a free bagel with cream cheese, after getting me a magazine and a pillow. No contest: nowhere are you ever treated as good as in a plane.

Right there from the airport I called April to tell her I wasn't leaving for another day and that I'd meet her at *Give Her the Moon.* There was no answer, though. Of course part of me started thinking she was out with the Greek god, but another half made me figure she'd already left for *Give Her the Moon.* Wouldn't she be surprised if I came in and snuggled up next to her? And if she wasn't there, well, then, I could still see the movie.

So Mom dropped me off at the theater. Once I was inside, a quick look at the screen told me that I hadn't missed too much. I started searching the back rows where April likes to sit, but she wasn't there. Okay, I'd go to the front, stand to the side, and, when the movie was showing a real bright daylight scene, it'd light up the theater enough so I could see if she was there or not.

So I went up to the front of the theater, took a quick look, and saw, when a very bright scene lit up the place, April in the first row kissing the Greek god.

Of course I just stood there watching them. I murmured under my breath something stupid like, "Well, I'm not going to be able to pretend anymore." And while I felt my blood turn to boiling ginger ale, from a few rows back some guy yelled, "Hey, sit down, will you!"

April and the god stopped kissing to see who wasn't sitting down. When she saw me there, she looked surprised for a second, and then looked at me with hate. I knew she wasn't going to say, "I'm sorry," but I didn't expect what she did say:

"What, are you checking up on me?"

"No, my plane was grounded, and—"

"I'll bet."

"Call the airport."

"Hey!" the guy in the audience yelled. "Down in front!"

Next day, I turned down the bagel, pillow, and magazine from the flight attendant. I just wanted to look out the window at the clouds and think of what I could do. And during the few seconds I didn't think about April, I thought maybe I shouldn't tell Dad what had happened, and not just because I knew he'd feel really bad for me. Like he said to me a lot of times, "When you come to town, it's like a vacation for me, too," so I didn't want to ruin his vacation.

So I put on my best smile as I got off the jetway. I kept smiling when I half-heard him tell me how he'd gotten us a pair of tickets to two Broadway shows, and one ticket for me for Tom Petty and the Heartbreakers at Radio City Music Hall. "Bill," he said, "I knew you wouldn't want to be seen in a group of kids your age with someone my age. It'd look like I was taking you." He was so great about it I almost told him everything then and there.

That afternoon, we went to see a Broadway Show League softball game, where the stars from different plays and musicals play each other just for fun. I might have had some fun if I wasn't in such pain. *My Surfing Days* played *Theda Bara and the Frontier Rabbi,* two shows I saw and liked last year. Problem was, *Surfing* beat *Theda* 18–15 in an extra-inning game, so I had to cheer at plenty of runs, hits, and errors, even though I didn't feel like cheering anyone—especially the girl on the *Theda* team who looked phenomenal and had long, straw-colored hair.

That night, Dad and I went to Giants Stadium to see an exhibition game between the Giants and the Patriots, where Craig James—a big hero of mine—was great as usual, as great as he was during that famous game against the Dolphins where he scored two TDs during the final 42 seconds. But by this time I just couldn't cheer anymore. And though I didn't talk too much, and though he didn't ask what was wrong with me, Dad knew something was wrong.

But once we got back to the apartment, I snapped on the Yankees' late game with Seattle and turned the sound off. And when I looked at him, he looked into my eyes, and I could hear him saying, "Come on, tell me. Let me help."

I told him everything, finishing with, "When this happened to my friend Doug, he was able to say, 'I'll always love her, and we'll always be good friends.' But not me. I want April hit by a truck."

If I hadn't been so miserable, I know he would have laughed at that. But he knew I was joking because I didn't know what else to do. He gave me a big, tight-lipped, silent smile. Then he added, "Bill, I know it's going to be hard, but you're going to have to forget her."

"Forget her? Dad, I thought this was the girl I was going to love for the rest of my life."

He nodded in a way that showed he wasn't surprised to hear me say it. "Losing your first love's the worst."

"I wish I'd never met her."

Then he gave me a doubtful look. "Would you really rather not have had all those good times this summer? Weren't all the highs worth all the lows?"

"I don't know," I said, before deciding. "They'll only be worth it if she comes back."

"No," Dad said, sounding real definite. "Don't hope for that. Don't even think that way. You can't put your life on hold till April tells you it can go on. You've got to live for now. I know it sounds clichéd, but there will be others."

"Dad, I don't want anybody else. I want April."

He breathed out a long breath. "I know, Bill. Believe me, I know."

And I knew what he was talking about. When my mother fell in love with Allen, a guy I only half-remembered now, I thought I'd never forget the yelling there used to be over him.

"I used to think I'd never love anybody else again," he said. "But I have."

And he has. His new girlfriend Lorna is really great.

"And you will, too," he went on. "Only next time ask the girl questions when they occur to you. Whether you think so or not, you didn't ask her about the 'Greek god' because you were afraid of what you were going to hear."

It hurt to have him bring it out in the open like that, but I had to admit it. "You're right."

"One other thing," he said. "Don't hate yourself when you start doing some very stupid things. Every guy does when a girl he loves breaks up with him. You'll promise you'll never call her again, and then you'll call her again. You'll swear you'll never drive by her house again; you'll drive by her house again." Then he looked at me. "And no matter how many stupid things you do, I'll understand why you're doing them, because when you lose someone you love, you go through a period of something that's got to be at least a second cousin to temporary insanity."

(I didn't know it then, but he was right. When I got home, I did plenty of stupid things, and a lot of them more than once. I called her house so I could talk to her, and hung up every time she answered. I drove by her house to see if she was outside on zero-degree days when nobody in his right mind was going outside unless he had an emergency.)

"But," he told me, "in time, sanity returns. And some day, it will. Take it from one who knows, okay, Bill?"

Funny; he looked at me in such a way that I could tell that, yes, he was sad for me, but he wasn't worried for me. And just his thinking I was going to be all right made me believe that I might be.

"I'll be fine, Dad. I promise."

"Great," he said, extending his arms. And we hugged the way I let him hug me when we're all alone. Then he looked at me and smiled. "Don't look now, but Rasmussen has a no-hitter after five."

"I know! I've been paying attention!"

But when Rasmussen lost the no-hitter the very next inning, it seemed like a real bad omen to me.

When I got home, I have to admit I found out April wasn't a total rat. Lots of girls keep the guys' rings even after they've broken up with them, but when I got home, there was a package waiting for me. In it was my ring and the watercolor from Ongonquit. There was a note with it, too—typewritten, probably because, I remembered, April and I once had a talk about how typewritten letters just don't seem as romantic as written ones.

Dear Bill. Thank you for everything. Good-bye.

I read that little note over and over and over again, so much that I even started noticing that the *e* on her typewriter came out a little higher than the rest of the line. Hey, no matter where the *e* was, the last word in the note was still "Good-bye."

"This'll be the last girl I'll ever give my ring to," I told Mike and Doug. "That's it! I will *never* get involved with another girl again as long as I live. They're poison!"

They both nodded through all my ranting and raving, because they too knew what I meant. Mike had had his rough times with Mili ("She spelled it with one *l*," Mike said, "so she'd sound more delicate. She turned out to be about as delicate as the Chicago Bears' front four").

"I'll tell you one thing," Doug said, while undoubtedly thinking of Chris, the girl who'd dumped him, "a chick'd have to be the most beautiful thing in the world for any of us smart guys to take a chance on getting mixed up with a girl again."

"Right," Mike and I agreed. And we'd kept that promise. None of us had gotten stupid enough to get involved with another girl all year long.

But during all of autumn and half of winter there was one thing I never told Dad or Mike or Doug or Eddie: I felt more important when I was with April. I even think she got me the job at the hotel.

My Uncle Bob had gotten me the interview at the Quality Court; now it was up to me to get the job. And after that disastrous interview I'd had with

Honeywell (where I didn't get hired) to the good interview I'd had with Friendly's (where I did), I'd figured out a few things. I knew now it wasn't just the suit you were wearing, but also the tie, which should be quiet enough for a wake. I'd also learned that you get out of the office as soon as the boss stands up at the end (which I didn't do when I interviewed at Grenoble Mills, which I'm sure is why I didn't get the job).

And when Ms. Algarotti, the hotel manager, asked me a question, I didn't just answer her with a quick "Yes" or "No," but actually talked a little. I told her it'd be exciting to work in a hotel because I liked people, and this way I could meet them from all over the world. I didn't go on and on about it, and I didn't go into the routine about how I'd be one of the best employees they ever had in the 186-year history of the company (like I did at Shreve, Crump, & Low—another job I didn't get).

And so, the Quality Court interview was the best one I ever had, the absolute best. If before I'd gone in there I'd written down how I would have wanted it to go, I couldn't have imagined anything better than what actually happened in there. I really thought Ms. Algarotti liked me.

So I was really shocked when she didn't offer me the job.

No, she didn't. She said a little something about having to see other people, and that she'd let me know. Big difference from what happened after my interview at Rite-Way Dry Cleaners, when Mr. Hatfield did everything but throw me a surprise party. Or my Friendly's interview, which ended with Mr. Whitner standing up, smiling, shaking my hand, putting my name on a time card, and handing me a uniform.

This time Ms. Algarotti only did three of those five things. She stood up, smiled (it was a nice one, I'll admit it), and shook my hand—but she didn't say, "Congratulations!" and ask me what size blazer I wore. I left wondering what I'd done wrong that made her want to see someone else.

But the next day I was in Burlington Mall wandering around with April so I could get an idea of what she might like for her birthday—and who did we run into but Ms. Algarotti? I looked at her, she looked at me—and then she looked at April. I swear it, I saw it in her face: she admired me more because I was holding hands with a good-looking girl. If I was good enough to get someone like that to fall in love with me, she must have thought, I must be some kid.

If anyone thinks I'm crazy for thinking that, tell me why that night she called me and gave me the job. Sure, I might be wrong, but why do I feel I'm not?

3

Great! There was a parking space in the back lot. I'd be able to stop at Eddie's after all.

I slowed down just right so I wouldn't scare someone walking out the back door of DePasquale's or Tile Panorama. When I got out, Mike the Cop gave me an approving look.

Even before I got near Eddie's back door, I smelled the good news: It hadn't been long since Ed had pulled a tray of fresh doughnuts out of the oven. And sure enough, when I walked in, I saw Charlie, the guy who owns the hardware store, slapping his hands against each other up and down to get off the fresh sticky white stuff that makes a honeydip a honeydip. Dr. Millit, the dentist upstairs, was finishing a jelly-filled, and looked awfully happy.

Of course, there's another reason people come to Eddie's—it's a place you can talk.

"They're all stupid," said Dr. Millit.

Charlie waited until he'd swallowed to answer. "Not so stupid, Doc. Ed?"

Eddie, meanwhile, had just turned around from the coffee machine. I had to smile, because between his white hair and long beard and his "bowlful of jelly"

-belly, he kind of looks like Santa Claus to begin with—but when he's wearing his favorite red shirt, he really could pass for Saint Nick's twin brother.

Eddie was shaking his head and laughing. "How smart are athletes? I like what Pete Rose's wife said. 'The only book Pete Rose ever read was *The Pete Rose Story*.' " Then he laughed the funny Santa Claus way he does when he tells one of his own jokes.

Charlie was still shaking his head. "That doesn't mean anything. Reading books has nothing to do with being smart."

"Don't tell Bill that," Ed said, getting me into the conversation as soon as he could. (How many adults bother doing that?) "He's going to write books. What do you think, Bill? Average athlete stupid?"

"Well," I said, "when you see them interviewed, not many of them sound too bright."

"There you go," Ed said.

Charlie got off the stool. "We'll have to agree to disagree," he added as Dr. Millit finished his coffee. Then he snapped his fingers. "Let me bring home a half dozen for Louise. Pack me up six honeydips, will you, Ed?"

"Ah, honeydips," I repeated. "They're still," I said, "the best doughnuts east of the Mississippi and north of the Mason-Dixon Line." Ed handed me one, I took a giant bite, and smiled my satisfied-customer grin.

Ed gave me a mischievous look. "You ever been west of the Mississippi or south of the Mason-Dixon Line?"

"Never west of the Mississippi," I admitted, "but we drove to Virginia last year to meet some cousins.

I think that's south of the Mason-Dixon Line, isn't it?''

Ed smiled and shook his head that no, he didn't know. Charlie shook his head, too, to let us know he didn't know, either, as he took his half dozen and walked out with Dr. Millit.

''But,'' I said, holding up what was left of my honeydip, ''I can tell you that no doughnut I ate in Virginia—or in Connecticut, New York, New Jersey, Delaware, or Maryland on the way down—was as good as an Eddie's.''

''Some compliment,'' Ed joked, ''when you consider what passes for food at turnpike rest stops.'' Then he patted his big belly, and said, ''Yeah, I can't resist 'em, either.''

I smiled. ''You know what I wish you'd do?''

He gave me a suspicious look. ''If you're talking about me making those peanut-butter-and-cinnamon crullers you thought'd be good, once was enough.''

''No, I think you should film a TV ad so everybody'd know about your doughnuts!''

The sound of my exclamation point rang in the air, because all of a sudden it was very quiet. Eddie wasn't looking at me right then, and seemed to be thinking of how to answer me. Finally he did, and managed a smile.

''It is a good idea, Bill. I watch some of them commercials where guys like me are telling people to buy what they sell. I've thought about doing it.'' Then he shook his head and pointed to his eyes. ''But I wouldn't be able to handle any more business than I got.''

Eddie motioned me to the end of the counter, and I followed. He turned around to the cash register, reached behind where he keeps the mail, and took out an official-looking envelope.

"Bill, help me out here. How much does the Electronic Company want? I can see the little red guy pointing to the number, but I can't see the number. What is it?"

"Um, $184."

He nodded. "Thanks."

For a moment, neither one of us said anything. I just took another bite, hoping he'd say something. When he didn't, I tried to think of something to change the subject and not make it look like I was trying to do just that.

But then he said, "I tell you, if it wasn't for Mary Mulcahy, I wouldn't even be able to stay open."

I was confused. "Mary Mulcahy?"

He looked right at me. "You know a girl at your school named Mary Mulcahy?"

What I knew was that I had to get going right away if I was going to get to work on time, but I wanted to hear this. "Mary Mulcahy," I repeated. "Where have I heard that name?"

Ed nodded. "I asked her the other day if she knew you. She said the name rang a bell with her, too. She's a sophomore."

". . . I think there's a Mary Mulcahy in one of my studies."

"Kind of short, kind of cute . . . ?"

I shook my head no. "I wouldn't remember what she looks like. There are about a hundred kids in that study. But wait a minute, what does she have to do with you keeping the shop open?"

"Because," he said, pushing the napkin holder a little toward me, just wanting to do something with his hands, "it isn't easy to get to here from Linden unless you drive. If I had to depend on public transportation, I'd have to get up three in the morning to get here in time to open. The T doesn't run too much that time of night."

"So Mary Mulcahy drives you?" I guessed.

He gave one big, definite nod. "Every day."

That stopped me midbite. "Every day?"

"Every day," he said, letting me know he wasn't making a mistake about it. "She gets me in here by 6:30. Parks in the parking lot out back, then walks to school, 'cuz they don't let kids park in the school lot, I hear."

"Right . . ."

"Then after school, she walks over to the library where she works. Then when she gets out," he said, going into a singsong voice, "she walks back and gets me and I close. She's only missed once in the, what, the six months she's been doing it."

"Six months?"

Ed nodded again. "Six months. She says the shop's on her way in, and she likes to get to school early, anyway. Says it's no big deal. But," he said, pointing a finger, "it is."

"Yeah, it sure is."

Ed's watch beeped out that it was four. Even though he keeps it seven minutes fast, I knew I had to get out of there.

And so did Ed. "Look at that, I been doing all the talkin'. Tell me—how you doing?"

"Okay."

"Tomorrow," he said with a sincere finger point, "we talk about you."

I grabbed the last of the honeydip. "I'd better get goin'."

"All right, Mr. Bill," he said, giving me a little

military salute left over from his Navy days. "See you tomorrow."

If he could mention a TV-rerun star, so could I. "Tomorrow, Mr. Ed."

My car started right away, probably because I'd forgotten to worry about it before I put the key in. And the reason I forgot was because I was still half knocked out from what I'd just heard.

My God! Every day for six months! *Every* day!

If this Mary Mulcahy was the kid who was in my study, I wanted to go up to her Wednesday and tell her how terrific she was. I hadn't forgotten that article I read in the *Globe* that proved how lousy people feel when they retire—that some even die because they feel like they have nothing to live for. I was pretty grateful, then, to this Mary for helping out my friend Eddie so he wouldn't have to give up his shop and all the friends he liked seeing when they came in there.

And then I got an idea.

4

My idea kept me awake an extra hour or two. But at least I wasn't kept awake because of April.

When I got to school, I didn't go straight to the *Dallinews* office the way I always do, but over to the sophomore homerooms. No one was in 205, no one in 204. The lights in 203 and 202 weren't even on yet.

But they were on in 201, so I peeked through the door, not wanting her to see me. There was one kid in the room in the second row, second-to-last seat—a girl I did recognize from my Wednesday third-period study.

She was doing her homework, I guess, and had her head down, so I couldn't make out too much of her face. But I was able to notice that her hair was blonde. Not great-looking long and straw-blonde, like April's and Larah's, but . . . scraggly and white. Not as scraggly as Jeanne Gorman's, whose hair is so thin you can see the pink of her head right through her hair. Still, this girl's hair looked almost as wimpy.

I didn't think she looked like much in the light brown dress she was wearing. Maybe it was because she was sitting down, but, I don't know, I sort of got the impression that it didn't really fit her right, that it was too big on her. Even though Dallin's a private school, nobody has to wear uniforms—but still, this washed-out-looking brown dress had the look of some sort of uniform. An awful one.

Well, I thought . . . maybe this isn't Mary Mulcahy.

Then all of a sudden she looked up to see who'd come into the room—and caught me looking at her. She looked right back at me, and all I could think of was, let me get out of here. I turned around and just walked out fast. If there was one thing I didn't want, it was having this girl think that I was checking her out because I wanted to date her.

Whoa! I had to put on the brakes right away or I would've banged right into someone who was on her way into 201.

"Hi," I said, making it sound like nothing was out of the ordinary, nothing was wrong, seeing as it was a girl.

"Hi."

"Can I ask you a question?"

"Sure," she said with a smile (a pretty one).

"Thanks. Do you know—"

I never got to say, "Mary Mulcahy?" because right then I saw the books she was carrying in front of her. Right there on the one in front, on white adhesive tape, MULCAHY was written in ballpoint pen. Eddie had said short and cute. He was just about right.

I said, "Um" as I tried to think of a question. Finally I could only come up with, "This is where the sophomore homerooms are, right?"

"Right," she said, giving me a look to let me know she was surprised I didn't know that, a look that let me know she didn't quite believe me.

"Thanks. Great," I said, starting to walk backwards away from this pretty girl who would have looked a lot more elegant if she didn't wear a blue denim shirt and gray corduroy chinos. "Thanks," I said again, as she started looking at me like I was crazy. I turned around and sped up to get to the exit door a little faster, which must have made me look crazier.

I might sound like I worry too much. But one thing I've learned the last three years: At a small, private school like Dallin, everybody knows everybody else, and everyone talks about everybody else, too. I wouldn't want it getting around I was hanging around the sophomore house checking out the tenth-graders. That's another thing I should have learned by now—you try to do something secretly, without anyone noticing, and you might as well be wearing a sign and sending out press releases in advance.

And if I'm going to be really honest, I have to admit I wouldn't want it getting back to April that I was interested in a sophomore, either. It's always a step down if the girl you go out with is younger than the last one you had. If a sophomore was all I could get, that said something about me—that I couldn't think too much of myself, not if I went out with anyone that young. Not if she wasn't at least as beautiful as April was.

And Mary just wasn't. Sure, she was pretty, but she didn't take my breath away like April did when we fell in love at first sight. Wearing clothes that looked like they came right out of an L. L. Bean catalog didn't help, either, at least not with me. They just weren't elegant.

Then I started feeling lousy about all these thoughts. It was *Mary* that really mattered, not what she looked like, right? It was one of the reasons I was going to suggest to the staff what I was going to suggest.

I walked into the office, where everyone was listening to Karen—another beautiful girl (with a great-looking boyfriend at Boston College). She had on a dress we all like: a dark green sweater-dress which makes her phenomenal figure stand out even more. And, I noticed again, letting her chestnut-brown hair get even longer was a really good idea, too.

". . . We're doing okay with the sophomore class," she was saying. "Sales are up almost ten percent . . ."

Lucky for us that Karen's our financial manager. In the two years she's been on the job, the paper's made more money, mostly because she's single-handedly gotten plenty of Ardmore store owners to realize that taking out an eighth-of-a-page ad wouldn't kill them, and might make their name a household word with Dallin kids. Half the store owners said they would've taken out ads years ago if somebody had only bothered to come around and ask them.

". . . but I'd really like it if we could get a story that'd help us break the circulation record set by the Class of '73. And nobody's come up with a good idea for a new column yet. What can we do?"

Was that my cue, or what? I raised my hand.

"Bill?"

Mike, Luke, and Doug had all had their backs to me, so they hadn't even realized I'd walked in. Now they turned; I took in their faces before delivering.

"It's not an idea for a column, but it's an idea."

"Okay, great—what?"

I leaned against the computer table and got comfortable. "Karen, yesterday we were all in here talking about how we don't think Larah Lavery is so outstanding."

And Karen looked like she'd been waiting for months for this discussion to come up. "You mean you guys don't think that Larah Lavery is particularly outstanding?"

"Nope."

"Uh-huh."

"No."

"None of us do."

"Well," Karen said, lifting up her arms and then letting them fall against her sides, "I am *so* glad! I've always thought you guys were all taken in by her, too." We all shook our heads no. "I mean, I didn't want to say anything because everyone in town seemed to think she was so great, but if we're really going to be honest—"

"That's what we're really going to be," Mike said.

"Well, then! I'll tell you what drove me crazy—Larah onstage didn't look like the Larah we all see around the halls. Where was all her makeup? Or the little white boots with the pink tassels? And," she said, delivering the knockout punch, "where was the trademark black nail polish?"

"She wasn't wearing it?" Luke asked.

I shook my head no. "I thought it was something I should mention in my story, but every time I finished writing and started to reread, the line 'Larah wore clear nail polish instead of black' kept sticking out like a sore thumb—"

"—with black nail polish on it," Mike, my buddy with the same sense of humor, said along with me.

"Tell her the elevator story," Doug said.

I didn't want to. "I'd rather tell her my idea."

"Yes, do. What's your idea?"

I smiled. "The Miss *Inner* Beauty Contest."

Luke squinted in a way that let me know he didn't think it was such a good idea. But Doug's eyebrows went up higher than usual, Karen's mouth opened and formed an "O," and Mike snapped his fingers. "The Miss *Inner* Beauty Contest! Yes!"

Karen was quickly nodding away. "For a *real* Outstanding Young Woman. It sounds good," she said. "*Real* good!"

So I told them all about Mary Mulcahy. They were blown away by it.

"Whattt?"

"She drives him in every day?"

"Since school started?"

"That early in the morning?"

"*Every* day?"

I just kept nodding and nodding and nodding through every question they flung at me and always looked them in the eye to let them know for sure I wasn't lying. Finally Doug made a face. "She probably just does it to get free doughnuts."

"I don't think so," I said, cracking my knuckles, though I hadn't thought about that before.

"Well, if that isn't the reason," said Mike, rubbing behind that right ear of his that sticks out a little, "she's an Inner Beauty, all right."

"A definite nominee," Karen said.

Mike was nodding up and down. "Hey, give the girl the prize right now."

"Like they say, it's a little early to project a winner," said Doug, who watches those election returns on TV every November. "Though she might win because you might not get anyone else in the school who's got any Inner Beauty to speak of."

"Ohhhh," Karen said in the tone she uses whenever Doug gets a little too suspicious. "I'm sure there are plenty of inwardly beautiful kids around."

"At least to give us a Final Four," Mike said. "But no matter what happens, we know we've got someone strong—"

"—a strong candidate—"

"—right, who's done something good enough to be Miss Inner Beauty."

I'd noticed that one of us hadn't been saying very much. "Luke, what do you think?"

Luke still shook his head no. "One thing's bothering me, though."

"Yeah?"

"Yeah, what?"

He gestured with both his arms. "Is it going to be one of those contests where girls walk around in their bathing suits? Because I don't want to see a lot of arf-arfs walking on a stage, you know what I mean?"

"Ohhhhhhhh," Karen said, angry he was making fun of not-so-good-looking girls.

"Who says," I argued, "that kids with Inner Beauty don't have Outer Beauty, too?"

Luke gave me a be-serious look. "Yeah? When? No offense, Karen, you're an exception, but the nicest girls are never the good-looking ones."

We never got to debate that one, because Doug tapped me on the shoulder to prepare me for the question he was going to ask. "So what does this Mary Mulcahy look like?"

"She's pretty," I said in a definite voice so they'd know she was. "Maybe even very pretty." I decided not to mention that she liked to dress like she was about to go on a hike through the Himalayas.

Maybe I should have. "Sounds like you really like her," Mike said with a grin.

"Yeahhhh, Richards," Luke droned. "You going to get hooked up again with someone?"

"It's nothing like that. Leave me alone," I said, letting them know I didn't find any of this too funny. "You wanted a new idea, I gave you one."

"That's right," said Karen, getting excited again. "This is it!" She put out her hands wide. "This is the idea that gets us on *Local Focals*."

"Hey, that's right!" Luke said. "*Local Focals* loves stuff like this."

Right then we all got excited, too. Okay, being on *Local Focals* can't compare with sitting between Johnny Carson and Ed McMahon on the *The Tonight Show*—it is just a show you see in Boston—but there aren't too many people in town who do anything else between 7:30 to 8:00 every weeknight but watch this magazine show about the niftiest, craziest, most interesting things that go on around Boston.

"All right," Doug said. "So when are we going to have Miss Wonderful's Coronation? All Saints' Day has already gone by."

Karen didn't even hear him. "And *then*," she said, "we could get this to go nationwide. A Miss *America* Inner Beauty Contest. If we get enough publicity, we'll get the day we do it put on the calendar as National Inner Beauty Day—a celebration for nice people! And," she said, outstretching her arms wide, "we'll make a video!"

"Let's get to work," I said.

Writing the whole announcement only took us five minutes:

ANNOUNCING DALLIN HIGH'S MISS INNER BEAUTY CONTEST!

DO YOU KNOW A GIRL WHO'S DONE SOMETHING NICE? A GIRL WHO'S DONE A *REALLY GOOD* GOOD DEED? THEN WRITE A LETTER AND NOMINATE HER FOR THE MISS INNER BEAUTY CONTEST!

We'll print the four best letters here in *Dallinews*. (If you want, sign yours "Name Withheld.") Then, after you read all four on the ballot we'll have in our next issue, we'll ask you to vote for the girl you think should be

MISS INNER BEAUTY!

She'll be given such prizes as:

- A 25-lb. box of chocolates from Ardmore Candy
- A bouquet of roses from Ardmore Florist
- A $25 gift certificate from Cathedral Groceries
- A $25 gift certificate from Salon D'Ardmore
- A $25 gift certificate from Farrington's (Good for records, cassettes, or CDs)

at

THE AWARD CEREMONIES TO BE HELD SATURDAY, MARCH 17TH AT O'GORMAN HALL. (Tickets: $3)

SO NOMINATE YOUR CANDIDATE FOR MISS INNER BEAUTY NOW!

"What do you think?"

"Great," Mike said. "Now you get to work writing a letter nominating Mary."

My first reaction was to say, "Ohhhhh, no. Ohhhhhhhhhh, *no*." But I knew it had to be me. Who else was the most logical person to write it? I was the one who'd discovered her.

"Okay, okay. I'll write it up during study today."

The study Mary was in, in fact.

5

When the bell rang for third period, I took the route past the home ec rooms. I'd been going this way ever since school began—because if I went the other way, past the junior rooms, I might run into April accidentally.

Funny thing was, I'd found out that going this way saved me some time. The home ec classes take a lot of double periods, so kids don't change as much between classes, and that makes the halls a lot less crowded.

Of course, I would have rather been late for every class and even risked getting suspended if I could have had April back.

I walked in at the back of the study and looked around for Mary. It was just at that moment that she walked in the front of the room, wearing her which-way-to-the-great-outdoors outfit. If she had been my sister, I would have liked the way she looked, and even would have offered to go camping with her some weekend. But as a girl . . .

Mary kept standing at the front of the room, looking at the guy she remembered from this morning. She smiled at me, and I didn't know what to do but look embarrassed.

Then we heard a booming voice: "Is there a problem, Mr. Richards?" Don't think that two kids standing up and not sitting down didn't bother Mr. Aronson, a teacher who has a heart attack every time kids don't get into seats the second they walk through the door.

Every kid in the room, of course, had to turn and look at us.

"—Mr. *Richards*—"

I just l-o-v-e teachers who always come down hard on the boy and never say a word to the girl. "No, there's no problem, Mr. Aronson."

"Then," he said, lowering his glasses all the way to the tip of his nose (which is his way of letting you know he thinks you're as good as a speck of dust), "would you two kindly take your seats so you won't continue disturbing us?"

Yeah, I wanted to say, we're really *disturbing* everyone. All these kids who've been able to get through every part of *Friday the 13th* won't be able to get over the shock of seeing two kids standing up in a room instead of sitting down. Pretty soon they're going to be shaking like they've all been possessed by the Devil.

But how can you win with teachers, especially ones who should have retired at 35, when everything about kids starts bothering them? I muttered a few sounds that made it sound like I was sorry, but I half-expected he'd make me repeat them louder so everybody could hear me-the-kid apologize to him-the-adult. Credit where it's due, he let it go.

I started down the first row to get the one seat there, even though I always hate being as close as that seat was to the front of the room. Only problem was, of course, Mary wanted to sit down fast, too, and was going for the same seat.

"Um," I said.

"Um," she said.

"You take it."

"No, you—"

"You—"

"Sit. Down," boomed Aronson, so loud that the kid in the second row moved right over in a panic to an empty seat in the third row. "Here's a seat," she said in a worried voice, and then I noticed she was the sophomore I thought was Mary earlier before I almost bumped into the real Mulcahy. The kid moving because she was so scared of Aronson made Mary and me look at each other, and we had to laugh.

"Will. You. Two—!"

End of laugh. Mary slid into the sophomore's old seat and I plopped myself in the one behind her in the first row. Finally, after everyone stopped looking at us, I pulled out my spiral notebook.

Okay, let's get this over with.

Dear Editor: The girl I know with the greatest inner beauty is Mary Mulcahy.

Then I stopped for a second to "organize my thoughts," as Ms. Naiman's taught me to do. What was the main point that I wanted to get across? That Mary had to get up at 5:30 in the morning to take Eddie in.

And while thinking for a few secs, I looked up from my paper, started tapping the top end of my pen against my bottom lip, squinted a little, things like that, and, without even thinking, started looking at Mary. It wasn't more than two seconds before she sort of straightened up a little in her chair. And somehow *I* knew that that meant *she* knew I was looking at her.

But I didn't realize it quick enough. She turned her head, looked at me, and saw from my face that, yes, I had been looking at her. I swear she could even see that I was thinking about her. And while I never blush (red cheeks in winter, yes, but blushing, never) I have a feeling that just then I was as red as Eddie's favorite shirt.

Now I'm not an expert on smiles, but I have a feeling I could read what Mary's said. What's more, I didn't like what I was reading. Her smile said, I get the feeling you want to get to know me better—and I'm smiling so you'll be able to see that I think that'd be great.

I put my head down so fast I almost got whiplash.

Never mind "organizing my thoughts." I just wrote Mary's story real fast and—of course—signed it *Name Withheld*.

And to make matters worse, when study was over, even though I took the home ec route, I ran into April—with her friend Larah.

What were they doing in this part of the school?

What were they doing? They were walking along, talking and laughing like they owned the whole school, taking big steps with their little white ankle boots with pink tassels. And, in a way, I thought, these two beautiful girls did own the school. They could have any boy they wanted.

I stood there stopped in my tracks, just watching the guys walking in front of me who were walking toward them. Sure enough, a second after they passed these two goddesses, they turned around right away so that they could catch a view of their other wonderful sides, too.

Meanwhile, I wanted to turn around and run the

other way. But I couldn't, it was too late, they'd already seen me. They'd probably both guess I'd turned because I saw April coming, and I didn't want that.

But as she was coming closer, closer, I wondered what I was going to do. Should I say "Hi" first? Should I wait for her to say it first? Would she? Did I want her to? What if—

"Hi, Bill," she said, with a no-hard-feelings smile sort of framed by big earrings with feathers on them. She gave me a little wave, which is when I was able to notice her black nail polish.

"Hi," I said, smiling, too—but real angry inside. Sure, there were no hard feelings on her part—*I* was the one who'd spent those days and nights feeling hurt, not her.

Meanwhile, Larah didn't say "Hi"—she just nodded. And by the time they passed me and kept talking away like they'd never seen me in the first place, I stood there wondering if Larah ever told April not to go back with me, that she should stay with the Greek god. Or that if April breaks up with him, her boyfriend's got lots of friends at Boston College.

True, I knew I couldn't blame Larah for keeping us apart, but when she and April get together to talk, like when they're coming home from a party or going to the ladies' room together, does April ever say, "I should have stayed with Bill"? And if she does, does Larah say, "Oh, don't be a jerk, no, you shouldn't have"?

I wondered about it all through my Spanish class, just like I wondered about the nail polish and the little white ankle boots with pink tassels. Maybe Mary's clothes weren't so bad after all.

6

Kids who like to write love to talk, too, so whenever the *Dallinews* staff gets together, it's impossible for any of us to keep quiet for long. But we were quiet when we sat and read the letters nominating M.I.B. candidates, what we now called the contest for short.

For one thing, we didn't really expect so many letters. When you consider there are only about 300 kids who go to Dallin, and that only 193 of them subscribe to the paper, getting 77 kids to write and nominate a Miss Inner Beauty struck us as pretty good.

Finally, though, we were so impressed at what we were finding out about the girls at Dallin that we had to start talking. The only difference was that instead of speaking real fast like we usually do, we read the letters softly and slowly.

" 'Lora Sobolow,' " Karen read, " 'works at the Mayor's Voluntary Action Center two days after school every week and doesn't get paid. She works the switchboard and takes down the information when people call up. Then she also has to call sick kids' mothers to remind them if the kid has a doctor's appointment tomorrow. She calls people who live in old-age homes and reminds them to take their medicine, too. Best of all, she even helped get a kid adopted once, because she told her neighbors next door about a kid who needed a foster home. The neighbors took the kid in and liked him so much they adopted him.' Signed, Valerie Johnson."

" 'Joan Ronan,' " Mike read, " 'volunteers where I do, at the Medford Street Shelter for the Homeless. There are a lot of us kids working here. We pack little bags of food and help to pass them out to the people, but Joanie's special because she tries to get to know the people, too. I keep remembering one thing she said to me: "I don't just want to give food to the people—I want to sit and talk to them, too. I can tell a lot of them need that." Since she said that to me, I've been doing more talking to the people here, too. I think Joanie's taught me how to be a better volunteer, and that's why I'd vote for her for Miss Inner Beauty.' Signed, Joshua Fifer."

"Funny he didn't nominate his sister," Doug said. "Someone else did." He read, " 'Jennifer Fifer works at a place, I don't know the name of it, where kids come after school and hang around. A lot of these kids are from broken homes or families where nobody cares a lot, so at least this place makes them feel like they're welcome somewhere. Jennifer helped the kids there start a garden, and it's been going great.' " He looked up. "Joyce Hutchins wrote that one."

" 'Andrea Peloquin,' " I read, " 'works for Food for Survival. After school on Tuesdays and Thursdays, she stands outside the Stop 'n' Shop passing out fliers. These fliers say to shoppers that they should donate one of the items they just bought inside the store to the homeless fund. After Andrea's given out all the fliers, she stays around and empties the bins and packs the cans in boxes, too.' "

"Gee," Karen said quietly, "I've been in a lot of classes with her, but I never knew that. She never said anything about it."

"Guess she wouldn't be a Miss Inner Beauty if she had," Luke said. "And here's something I didn't know about Sandra Flynn." Luke's not the greatest reader, but he gave it his best. " 'Once a year every year Sandra Flynn takes some poor kids to the aquarium, and every Arbor Day drives them to Concord to go apple picking.' "

And so it went:

" 'Carol Hoidra works at the Ardmore Soup Kitchen most Saturdays. She's convinced the cook to try some different varieties and flavors, so the people coming there can have something new to look forward to.' "

" 'Julie Gould should be Miss Inner Beauty because she got the Next Move Theater to do a free show there.' "

" 'Allison McMullen works at the Home for the Blind every Sunday, reading to the people there.' "

" 'Marta Cassells goes grocery shopping for an old woman every Friday.' "

" 'Suzanne Foisy helped a lot during Clean-Up Day at the Belmont Community Center. Everybody was there four hours, she was there six.' "

" 'Charla Craig delivers groceries to senior citizens who live in apartments and can't get out and shop on their own anymore—every Saturday morning.' "

" 'Martha LaGrassa taught an old person who never learned to read how.' "

" 'Maureen MacDermott volunteers at Symmes Hospital and does all the boring jobs, pushing the carts down the corridors and sorting the clothes in the thrift shop.' "

" 'Janice Traganos helps out a family who came over here from Haiti, and baby-sits the three kids every Monday and Thursday nights so the kids' mother can work.' "

" 'Linda Cataldo has a 17-year-old friend (I can't tell you who) who had a baby. The friend doesn't have much money, so Linda baby-sits the kid for free.' "

Then came one of those moments when everybody was reaching for a new letter to read and we all caught each other's eye. That's when I could see from the serious looks on everyone's faces how impressed we'd all been. I knew some of the parents of these girls kids had written about, and some of them weren't super-rich. Some of them, like mine, find it's pretty hard to come up with the tuition. But these kids still did a lot of work for nothing to help people who were worse off.

"You know what else is going to be nice?" I said to the staff. "Once we print these letters, we're going to be giving a lot of other kids ideas on how to help people who need it."

Karen nodded. "We'll let even more people know what's going on if we get on *Local Focals*."

Mike raised his can of Dr. Pepper. "So let's give a toast to the guy who started the whole thing. To Bill Richards!"

"Bill Richards!" they all echoed. "Yeay, Bill!"

The whole thing embarrassed me, but I found myself feeling something else entirely when Luke picked up a letter and said, "Here's a letter nominating April Koral.'' I felt myself freeze, but I got ahold of myself as fast as I could.

Mike knew what I wanted to know, though. ''Who wrote it?''

'' 'Name Withheld.' ''

''Figures.''

''But,'' Luke said in a voice that boomed almost as much as Aronson's, while holding out the letter for all of us to see, ''whoever wrote it puts little circles over her *i*'s.''

We all rushed over to Mike to check it out for ourselves.

''There isn't a heart at the end of the sentence,'' Doug joked.

''Well,'' I said, ''don't bother going to look for Jeff Lonergan and the wrong-number message in his wallet. That's Larah's writing.''

''Brings up a good point,'' Mike said. ''Before we run anything on any of these kids, we're going to have to check out every girl nominated and make sure they've all done everything everybody says they have.''

Luke raised a finger. ''Check and make sure nobody signed letters with names like Chuck Waggon or Frank Furter.''

''Or,'' Mike smiled, ''my all-time favorite, Anne Chovy.'' But then, sounding like the son of an insurance man that he is, he got serious right away again. ''We've got to investigate every one of these claims to make sure they're real.''

''Right,'' said Doug.

''Bill, we know your girl's okay, since the guy she drives in told you she does it every day.''

I had to stop him right there. ''Uh, I wouldn't exactly say she's 'my girl.' ''

"You know what I mean," he said, annoyed I was making something out of a phrase he'd only thrown out. "But everybody else," he said, holding up an entry blank and waving it in the air like it was a check he didn't trust, "has got to be checked."

"I'll check 'em out," snapped Doug in a way that right away made us stop worrying whether or not the girls were legit—we'd soon find out what was what, thanks to our investigative reporter.

"Guess we'd better check 'em all out," Karen said.

"Listen to this one," Luke yelled. " 'I nominate Larah Lavery for Miss Inner Beauty, and to make sure she has some, I volunteer to take her into the biology lab some night when there's a full moon and take some real good X-rays.' "

"Yeah, but it is interesting, isn't it," Mike asked, "that nobody seriously nominated the 'Outstanding Young Woman' for Miss Inner Beauty?"

"Our 'outstanding young woman' isn't considered so outstanding by kids who really know her."

"Too bad we couldn't let those 'outstanding' judges know that."

"Can't we tell them now and demand a recount?"

It was just then that I found a letter that made me say, "Wait-wait-wait."

"What?"

"What?"

"What?"

"Tell us!"

"Listen to *this*," I said. "The kid who wants to X-ray Larah isn't the only one nominating her." I started reading, " 'I think Larah Lavery should be Miss Inner Beauty because she plays piano at the senior-citizen holiday dinners when we have dances there, and played Mrs. Claus for the Salvation Army delivering toys at Christmas. Name Withheld.' "

"Well, that sounds nice," Karen admitted.

"She probably plays just to hear people applaud and tell her how great she is," Doug snored.

"But here's the big thing," I said, trying to keep my voice from going higher. "Notice that in every word with an *e* in it, the *e* is a little raised up at the bottom, not on the same line as the other letters?"

"Yeah . . ."

"Well, let me tell you who owns this typewriter."

And after I did, Mike said, "Now here's what I want to know—did Larah know that April was nominating her—"

"—and did April know that Larah was nominating *her?*"

"And what does it matter if they did?" I decided. "If they really do do these nice things, they should be in the running to be Miss Inner Beauty."

"Well, that's true."

"Yeah."

"Yeah."

Then I blurted out, "And if April gets chosen Miss Inner Beauty, I'm moving to North Dakota."

Mike shook his head. "No, it's still going to be Mary."

I wasn't so sure. I hoped so, but I wasn't so sure. "Some of those other kids we got letters on have done some pretty nice things, too."

Mike shook his head no. "Twice a week, once a week, some once a month. Mary does her good deed twice a day, and has to be at this guy's doorstep at five-thirty every morning, and she almost never misses. You wait and see. It's going to be Mary."

7

Wanting to leave school soon as the bell rings is one thing, wanting to leave school soon as the bell rings on Friday is another—but wanting to leave school soon as the bell rings on the Friday before winter break and having to stay around to get out an issue is worst of all.

Mike was good, though, in keeping from saying, "If we don't get it to the typesetter by five, we might not get it back in time to sell it Monday morning after vacation." He knew we all knew that, and that we were all working as hard as we could.

Doug wiped his forehead and said, "I'm not just being dramatic when I wipe it, either. I really am sweating, and I still have four more M.I.B. letters to proofread. Where's Karen when we need her?"

And like a moment out of a movie, it was right then Karen came bursting in through the door like she was Grete Waitz ripping through a marathon finish line.

"Get ready," she half-screamed, "because I've got great GREAT news! I'm not going to drive you crazy by holding it in, either! Here it is!" She put her hands out and sung, "Double-U-Beeee-Zeee," just like the Channel 4 commercials.

We all knew what she meant and opened our mouths to shout, but Karen was even quicker. "Yes! That's right! Gerri Jontry's going to come and tape the M.I.B Contest for *Local Focals*! If everything comes out great, we'll get a whole seven-minute segment on the show!!"

"*Awwww-riiiight!*" Somehow the tired kids who'd just been sluggishly going over copy were replaced by electrified kids who were whooping and hollering. We jumped up and down and slapped our hands in high-fives.

"TV!"

"Wow!"

"Hey, Dallin High enters the Electronic Media Age!"

Karen was still the most stoked of all of us. "I'm going to call up Ms. Naiman and tell her! This'll help her get out of the hospital fast!"

Mike snapped his fingers. "Ask her something else, too! Ask her if we can postpone this issue till after vacation!" He looked at all of us. "Forget bringing what we have to the typesetter! We've got a whole new front-page lead story! Bill, you do the story. Luke, see if you can get some pictures of Gerri Jontry and anything else on *Local Focals*."

Luke and I agreed with a roar, and Karen started off to hit the closest phone booth. "Wait!" Mike called her back. "Don't say anything, don't *anyone* say anything about this. We're keeping it quiet until the paper comes out. It'll be a sure sellout that way!"

We gave out another roar, and Karen finally went off to call Ms. Naiman. But everything started calming down when Doug started wagging a finger at us.

I took a deep breath. "I know what that wagging finger means, Doug. What's wrong?"

"Well," he said, making sure we were coming back down to reality, "we've got a whole new set of what they call 'considerations.' Didn't Karen say they'll do seven minutes on the contest 'if everything turns out great'? Then our Miss Inner Beauty had better be able to handle being crowned on TV in front of camcorders taping her so she can be broadcast over half the state and on some of the stronger Rhode Island and New Hampshire stations." He leaned back in his chair. "Won't be much of a show if she can't. And I bet they don't run the tape if she isn't someone who can sell the contest."

It was Mike now who was raising his eyebrows the way Doug usually did. "Well, you do have a point." He looked at me. "What do you think, Bill? Can Mary Mulcahy handle the cameras?"

"And publicity?" Doug asked.

"Well," I said, "what if it isn't Mary who wins?"

They all squinted my opinion away.

"Mary's still going to win."

"Probably," Luke said, before upping it to, "Definitely, even."

"Name me one other kid who gets up at 5:30 every day when she could get up like two hours later."

Mike looked pretty serious. "What do you think, Bill? Can you imagine Mary getting up in front of the TV cameras and accepting an award?"

"Huh!" Luke snorted. "Can she even handle getting up in front of an auditorium full of kids to accept it?"

And the way the three of them were all looking at me, I knew for sure what they wanted me to do—go out with Mary to find out if she was future superstar material.

I knew the best defense is a good offense. I also knew I had to work fast. "I don't know," I said slyly. "Maybe it'd be a good idea if Karen went out with her, maybe for coffee or something, and see what she thinks."

Doug shook his head no. "But that isn't really going to prove all that much."

"Yeah," Luke chimed in. "Having Mary go out for coffee with another girl isn't too pressure-packed."

"Sure it is," I said. "Don't forget, Karen's a senior, and Mary's just a sophomore. If she can handle being with a senior girl she doesn't really know—"

Doug disagreed. "We'd know better if she went out with a guy," he said, trying to hide a smile. He was enjoying himself, I swear. "A senior guy'd be a good test."

Working fast hadn't worked. I decided to work slow and say nothing. Only thing was that by this time, everybody was saying nothing. The more they said nothing, the more that said to me.

"Bill," Mike finally breathed, "look—"

"All right," I decided. "I'll go out with her. As long as I can tell her that I'm on official business, that she's been nominated as Miss—"

"No, no, no, no, no," they all yelled at me.

"You can't tell her."

"Then she'll know she's been nominated."

"And she'll tell everyone about *Local Focals*."

I looked at all of them. "Well, if I ask her out, she's going to think I'm doing it because I want to go out with her. And I don't."

"Come on, Bill," Luke prodded. "You're the one who convinced us in the first place she's so great."

"I'm through with girls," I said. I looked at Mike.

"Just like you're through with girls, and"—looking at Doug—"*you're* through with girls. Luke, maybe you should do it."

He shook his head no. "Laura wouldn't like that."

I made a face. "Tell her it's for the newspaper."

"Heyyyy," he answered. "You think she's going to believe that?"

"Tell you what," Doug decided. "Let's flip for it. Everybody take out a coin." He reached into his pocket. "The one who doesn't match asks out Mary."

It sounded like a good suggestion to Mike, who started digging into his pocket, but it didn't sound so good to me. This was the girl who'd been so great to Eddie! How could I let the kids treat her like this? What were we going to do next, check out her teeth by having the kid open up her mouth like a horse? I'd started this whole thing because I wanted to see her get some sort of reward. And now look at what was happening.

"Hold it, hold it, hold it," I said as they got their coins ready. "I'll take her out."

"You sure?" said Doug.

"You don't have to," Mike offered.

"But," I told them, "it's only going to be after school for coffee."

Still, I was wondering, what was I going to say to her? How could I ask her out without having her think I was asking her out—when asking her out was exactly what I was doing?

8

Riiiiinnnng!

By the time the bell rings in Room 64 to end Wednesday third-period study, I'm usually already up and on my way out. Like everybody in that class, I know the thing rings when the tip of the second hand reaches 4.

But I just watched Jimmy Lentz, Dick Minogue, and everybody else get up when the second hand reached 3 as Aronson gave them dirty looks. I sat there because I was going to have to hang around for Mary.

I'd postponed it for as long as I could. The whole week of vacation, I didn't call her. I mean, even though I didn't want anyone to flip a coin over her, I wasn't going to call her up at home, because that would really make it seem like a date.

And when I dropped by Eddie's, I didn't mention anything to him about it, either. Somehow no matter what I said about taking her out just for the paper, I think he would have gotten the wrong idea, that I wanted to ask Mary out because I was interested in her as a girlfriend.

So I'd ask her right after the Wednesday study.

Monday morning, the guys and Karen were a little antsy I hadn't done it yet, but I told them if they didn't like my timetable, any one of them could ask her out. They shut up.

And right there after study, I got a good break. Mary had been in the middle of doing some homework and unlike us guys hadn't been noticing the clock. Everybody was clearing out, but she was just getting started to get everything together.

I was glad she didn't have any friends in the class she'd be walking out with. That's all I'd need—a couple of other girls hanging around making it even harder. But I got another good break, because the only kid left in the room was me. No one would have to see me do this, and word wouldn't spread and become the next big Dallin rumor.

Mary was hurrying now so she could get out of there and be on time for her next class. I noticed she was wearing a pink shirt today—a girl's shirt, not a boy's, but still something you'd call a shirt and not a blouse. Her corduroys this time were black.

"Arrrghhh!" she said, dropping a book. I just naturally swooped over to pick it up for her, and didn't think enough in advance of how I'd feel when I was face-to-face with her.

But there we were, face-to-face.

I noticed her eyes, which is something I usually never notice. With Mary, though, I couldn't help it. They were kind of green and flecked with little sprinkles of gold. They were different, maybe in a pretty way.

Anyway, I gave her the book. "Gee, thanks," she said with a big smile that showed me she'd worn braces when she was a kid.

"Um, ah, you're welcome." And even though I'd

gone over in my head what I'd say to her for ten whole days, all of a sudden I didn't know what to say. Besides, even a nondate like this still counted as asking out a girl, and I hadn't had much experience asking girls out. I never needed to, not after that magical first night with April.

Meanwhile Mary kept looking at me, and now I wasn't sure if I liked those eyes or not. I said nothing for what must've seemed like an hour and a half, even though I could see she wanted me to say something. I couldn't blame her for finally walking away, though not before giving me another smile.

It got me going, though. I followed her out, and when I caught up to her walking alone in the hall, give her credit—she knew I had to be walking next to her for a reason. She also must've figured out I was having trouble trying to think of something to say, so she tried to help and get things going.

"I'm Mary Mulcahy," she said, kind of brightly, giving me a hint as to what my next line could be.

"Hi, Bill Richards."

"Yeah, Eddie Petrucci told me about you."

Make it sound casual, Richards. "Eddie, yeah. Great guy, huh?"

"Oh, *yeah*. Great guy."

"Hey, how did you ever get to know him, anyway?"

She nodded, like she was telling me she thought it was a good question. "We used to live next door to him a long time ago. He brought over chocolate frosted doughnuts the night I was born—least that's what they tell me. I sure remember him bringing them over when my sister was born."

Here was my chance. "Um, why don't we go there after school and have one? Or more than one, if you want.'' That last line was one I never practiced—and it sure sounded it.

For a second I didn't think she was going to make it easy. ''Oh, noooo,'' she said, patting her stomach. ''I don't eat doughnuts.'' But then she said, ''Maybe somewhere else?''

I wanted to go to Eddie's, figuring if we went there, we could all talk together, and it'd be even less like a date. But somehow I got the impression she kind of knew that. Was this why she wanted to go somewhere else?

And then from behind me I heard, ''Hi, Mary!''

''Hi!''

''Hi!''

Two girls, sophomores, had shown up. I could see right away from their eyes and sparkling smiles that they were real happy to see a senior talking to their friend. I'm not trying to brag, but when you're a senior and look it, sophomore girls are of course automatically more interested in you than if you're a junior, and a lot more interested in you than if you're a sophomore and look it—which is why these girls were giving Mary a look that said, honey, you've won a prize bigger than any spin on *Wheel of Fortune*.

To make matters worse, after Mary had introduced me to Julie Mulroy and Marie de la Palme, she had to go and say, ''Bill, where should I meet you?'' You could almost see Julie and Marie hold in their breath.

''I got some stuff to do first,'' I half-mumbled. ''Meet me right by the side door near the parking lot at quarter to three.'' I made it sound more like a command than a request for a date.

''Quarter to three, then,'' she said very sweetly, acting like she was in control of the whole thing.

Meanwhile I walked away hoping that anyone who ever knew anything about me and April was nowhere near to overhear any of this.

And when I got to the side door at 2:47—taking my time just to be on the safe side, making sure nobody'd be around—there was Mary waiting.

"Hi!"

"Hi," I said a little softer, hoping by being calm I'd let her know she shouldn't get that excited. "You want to take my car, or should we take yours?" Sure, I knew hers was at the parking lot behind Eddie's, but I didn't want her to know that I knew that much about her.

"No, let's take yours."

Walking to my car wasn't the greatest, because I'm not too good at walking next to people I don't know and talking at the same time. With my head turned all the time looking at the kid I'm talking to—and worrying about what I'm going to say next—half the time I don't even notice where I'm walking. I still have a scar on my shin from the time I was walking and talking with Roberta Johnston on our way to the seesaw and didn't notice Jeff Hochhauser's little red wagon.

But here I was in a situation where I'd just have to walk and talk. "Nice day, huh?"

"Real nice," she said.

Only thing, of course, is that talking about the weather really means you're hard up for something to talk about—and everybody knows it, too. I had to try something else. "What kind of car do you have?"

She almost stopped walking for a second—probably because that line had just come out of nowhere and had nothing to do with the weather. But then she smiled and said, "A '74 Mustang."

I laughed. "That's what I have."

"Good," she said. "I'll feel right at home!"

Thank God that that day I'd gotten a space at the end of Hemlock Street instead of the middle, so it didn't take us too long to get to the car. I opened the door for her, and was a little disappointed that once she was inside, she didn't reach over and pull open the inside lock for me. Well, okay then, she wasn't 100 percent Miss Inner Beauty, but that wasn't the point of this meeting anyway—this was a test for lights-camera-action pressure. And so far it seemed like she was handling the pressure a lot better than I was.

Especially when the car didn't start.

"Um, on mine," she offered, "if you jiggle the key a little, it really helps."

I gave her a half-smile, and it made her smile disappear. Poor kid probably thought I was saying, "I don't need your advice, thank you, and each car's different—"

"Of course, each car's different," she said.

"Well," I said, trying to sound nice about it, "let me try to jiggle it."

And so I jiggled the key in the ignition, feeling kind of stupid, worrying that I'd feel even more stupid if it turned out she was right after all. On the other hand, I'd be pretty happy if I found a trick I didn't know about that'd get my car going every day without giving me a big headache.

"Uhhhm," she said real slow, "I'll tell you what I mean by jiggling . . ."

She reached over, and when her hand touched mine, I just automatically moved away like I'd been hit by a laser. It made her lose her cool for a second, too—but she got over it faster than I did and just reached over to do the jiggling she'd set out to do.

"Pump the gas, too," she told me.

I did. Even so—I'm almost glad to say—her jiggling didn't work, either.

"Maybe we should take your car," I said, before trying it one last time.

"Well," she said a little sadly, starting to shake her head no, when Vrrroooom! My car cooperated.

"Yaaaaay!" she said, clapping her hands in a way that made me laugh. Some girls I've had in my car (especially guess who) used to sit with their arms folded looking real impatient every time my Mustang wouldn't do what it was supposedly put on this earth to do. And no girl had ever cheered when it started before.

I thought about taking her across the town line to Lexington, where nobody'd know me. But I had to get to the hotel, and she probably had to get to work too, so we didn't have much time. (And don't think I hadn't thought of that when I planned this nondate.)

"How about the Sizzler?"

"Sure," she said, agreeable as ever.

And it was like a four-second ride from where we were.

We got into the Sizzler parking lot and I pulled to a stop. Mary didn't wait for me to run out and open the door for her—she just got right out. I had to wonder if I'd made her mad or something, maybe by not talking more—but then when she opened the restaurant door for me, she said, "One good turn deserves another."

Yeah, I thought, she's going to be able to handle the pressure of *Local Focals*.

Inside I got another good break: The little sign said "Please seat yourself" instead of "Please wait for the hostess to seat you." Since we didn't have to wait, I headed us to a booth.

"Here okay?"

"Sure!"

I checked the little cards on the table to make sure there wasn't a minimum we'd have to pay. Good—all they were doing was advertising some strawberry shortcake and their new Girl Scout Cookie ice cream.

Then a waitress wearing a "Doris" name tag came over right away and gave us a suspicious oh-oh-I've-got-teenagers-on-my-hands-here look. I kept my cool and looked at Mary. "Coffee?"

"Iced coffee?" she said, with a let's-try-something-a-little-different spirit.

I hadn't thought about iced coffee since the summer. (Don't go thinking about the summer now, I told myself.) Iced coffee sounded great. I ordered it too. But then Doris nodded in that I-knew-these-stupid-kids-wouldn't-order-much-and-now-I-won't-get-a-big-tip look, so I thought I'd better add, "And strawberry shortcake. Mary?"

Mary shook her head real quick, like even the words *strawberry shortcake* might make her gain a couple of pounds. Doris half-closed her eyes, nodded, and walked away without a word.

And that left me alone with Mary.

So I was about to talk about Aronson or some other teachers—even though I know that talking about teachers has to be the second most boring thing you can talk about next to the weather. But then I didn't have to say anything at all, because Mary said, "Where do you work?"

"Where do I work? Um, the Quality Court on Mass. Ave. I'm a bellman/desk clerk," I said, not telling her that 90 percent of the time I did bag-carrying and the other 10 percent of the time Ms. Algarotti let me work the desk.

"Oh!" she said in an interested way. "What's the best thing about it?"

". . . What's the best thing about it?"

"Uh-hmm," she said, in a voice that let me know she knew there was nothing wrong with the question, that it was a pretty good one (which, I had to admit, it was). "Yes," she repeated. "What's the best thing about it?"

"Well," I said, desperately trying to think of something, "lots of things."

She didn't say anything right away, but I could tell she wasn't rushing me. It was like she was telling me, "It's okay. I'll wait. I know there are lots of things you could mention, but since there are so many, you just need a little time to think and pick out the right ones." And I had a little extra time when Doris flopped down our iced coffees onto the table.

"Oh," I eventually started, "we get in some famous people. Sheila E., Mr. T., and that group Cinderella? Conrad Bain and Faye Dunaway even stayed with us when they made a TV movie that'll be out next year."

"Were they nice?"

"Oh, yeah!" I said, as Doris slammed my shortcake on the table. "Some of these stars really know how to tip. I got ten bucks each from Prince, Sean Penn, and Henry Kissinger."

"Wow." And it was a simple "Wow" that showed me she was interested and impressed, but wasn't going to sound like a V-8 commerical. I sort of liked that.

"And," I continued, "I like the great free meals we get from Nick, the head chef. Veal parmigiana, steak tartare." I motioned to my shortcake. "Great desserts, too." Then motioning to the shortcake again, "Not even a little?"

She shook her head no—she wanted to talk. "I bet a lot of funny things happen in a hotel."

"Oh! Abso*lute*ly!" And I told her about the time John told me to take those bags that were waiting in the lobby up to 401 . . . but didn't mention that the guy who'd open the door would be a seven-foot Ashanti native dressed in bright gold tribal robes. "Can you imagine," I asked, "what it's like to be standing in front of a hotel-room door expecting some guy in a suit and tie to open the door—and meet a seven-foot Ashanti?"

She was laughing. "I can just picture the look on your face! And," she added, "what's the worst thing about working there?"

Hey, I thought, this "What's the best?" and "What's the worst?" business is a good trick to know about when you're talking to people. You can ask anybody you meet what's the best and worst things about their school, job, friends, *lives,* anything—you'll always have something to talk about.

"The worst thing? Without a doubt, when we're overbooked. That's when we take too many reservations for the rooms we have. There have been times we've had two hundred reservations—

"For how many rooms?"

"A hundred and thirty-five."

"*Uh*-oh."

I nodded as I scooped the shortcake. "You should

see people after they've traveled across the country—sometimes halfway around the world—and we have to tell them we're already filled up, we don't have any more rooms, and there isn't a hotel, motel, inn, bed-and-breakfast, anything anywhere for forty miles, so it's either a cot in the function room or the couch in the lobby. I've actually seen a guy tip over the cigarette machine, then stand on it and stomp all over it. Sure, you can laugh, but we'll always remember Mr. Fardall from Los Altos, California, who made getting cigarettes impossible for three whole days."

"And," she asked, once she finished laughing, "what do you do when you're not in school or working?"

Wow, this girl could get a job tomorrow working as an interviewer! She was going to have no problem handling the contest. "Well . . . um . . . I write a column for the school paper . . ."

"*Dallinews?*" She took a sip of the coffee, leaned back, then brushed back a bit of hair. "I've been thinking I'd maybe like to write for it, too," she said slowly.

Good! A chance for me to find out more about her. "Well, we're always looking for new ideas."

"Well . . . let's see. New ideas . . ." she said, picking up her spoon and taking a small bit of the strawberry shortcake after all. "You ever think about starting a column on 'The Most Embarrassing Things that Ever Happened to Teachers'?"

" 'The Most Embarrassing Things that Ever Happened to Teachers,' " I repeated, trying the column name on for size. "It sounds kind of good."

"Do you know Ms. Weingarten?"

"Sure, sophomore English. My friend Mike had her. Very short, kind of . . . heavyset. Always wears red." I kept out the part how most kids call her Beachball.

She nodded. "She's got this real funny story from when she used to substitute-teach. One winter she was subbing in Sturbridge, you know where that is?"

"Sure, Mass. Turnpike Exit 9, way out, western part of the state."

"Right! So she goes to this school she's never seen. Anyway," she said, putting down her spoon with a thunk to let me know she wasn't going to take any more cake, "after Ms. Weingarten parks her car, she goes walking across a field that was covered with lots of snow and ice." (Here Mary gestured with her left hand, and I almost said, "Watch out, you're going to tip over the iced coffee!" but in a second I saw I didn't need to, she and it were going to be all right.) "But all that snow wasn't over a field," she continued. "Ms. Weingarten went walking . . ." (This time she gestured with her right hand but again didn't knock anything over. Here was a kid who definitely knew just how far her arms could go without doing something clumsy and embarrassing. She'd be able to walk down the contest runway no problem.) ". . . walking, along—and all of a sudden she wasn't walking anymore."

I stopped shortcaking. "What do you mean, she wasn't walking anymore?"

Mary looked in my eyes and smiled. "She was in six feet of water," she laughed. "Turned out there was a pond under that field of icy snow. And there's still a pair of her glasses at the bottom of that pond."

She laughed out loud again, and so did I, as I kept picturing Beachball Weingarten in her red dress in the water, looking a little like a fishing bobbin. Then when Doris gave a filthy look to these two kids who were having a good time, we thought we'd better calm down.

"Or," Mary said in only a slightly lower voice, "how about a column that gives advice on how a kid can get a job? We could ask people in town—like, ummmmmm, you know, the manager of the K-Mart, or the foreman at the Shell station, or *Eddie*—what they look for in a kid, what they want, when they hire somebody."

"You know, that's a good idea, too," I had to admit. "I think you should definitely try writing for the paper." (I almost said "try writing for us" but I hate when people try to sound big like that, using *us* to people who aren't part of *us*.)

"Well," she said, giving me a smile, "this is my first year at Dallin—"

"Oh, yeah?"

"Yeah, just transferred this year. And I figured the seniors and juniors run things, and wouldn't want a sophomore around—"

"No, it's not like that!" I said, before adding, "Not really."

"But if you're saying there's room for someone else—"

"Sure. Besides, everybody's got to start sometime," I said, quoting Bobby Rubinger, who told me the same thing when he was the managing editor two years ago.

"All right," she decided. "I'll write up some of these ideas, give them to you, and you can let me know what everyone thinks."

"Sure!" (Then I suddenly realized I'd just agreed to see her again.)

Doris walked by and put the check on the table without even stopping. Mary looked at me. "All set?" I said, putting my hands on the table and lifting myself up, remembering for the first time since we'd sat down that I did have to get to work.

"Sure," she said, but in a quiet way. I wondered if she were sad that we weren't going to get more time together.

Like I said, I'm not so good at walking next to people and talking, so I didn't know what to say on the way to the car. Maybe Mary felt the same way, because she didn't talk, either. But somebody had to say something, so when we reached the car, I was about to start when she said, "I'm still trying to think of new ideas for the paper."

"I think you've done pretty good so far."

She smiled a thanks as I let her in the car. "Yeah, I've been thinking lately about doing something like that. I mean, as a career. A reporter, then maybe even an anchorwoman. I'd start out slow in someplace like Wheeling, West Virginia and work my way up to a big city like Providence."

I shut the door, and as I walked to my side, I felt great. I had no doubt now: Mary could handle *Local Focals* no sweat. I mean, she even thought about being on TV for a living! What other proof would anybody need that she'd be great for The M.I.B. pageant?

The car started, and before I began driving, she asked, "Um, could you do me a favor and just drive me to the library?"

"Sure."

"Thanks. Otherwise, I'd be late."

"How much do you work there?"

She nodded. "Four days. Two days for pay, two days volunteering."

Volunteering?! Eddie said she worked at the library and I assumed that meant for money. He didn't mention she did any volunteering. Too bad I didn't know that when I wrote the letter—then she really would have Miss Inner Beauty all sewn up! For a second I wondered if I could get this new info added to my nomination letter, but I knew I couldn't. The paper was going to be out in a day or so, it had to have been printed by now.

Meanwhile, I went on to the new conversational trick Mary had taught me: "What's the best thing about working at the library?"

She laughed, happy I thought enough of her idea to use it myself. "Well, we don't get too many famous people dropping in, that's for sure. But there's The Young People's Story Group. I read to the kids who aren't old enough to read yet. There's this theory that if you can get them to see there are good stories in books, they might want to learn to read quicker. But that's only the two volunteer days. How many days do you work?"

Not that I particularly wanted to talk about myself, but I still liked that she was trying to get the conversation back to me. It showed something nice and considerate about her.

"Four."

"Do you have to work on Thursdays?"

"Thursdays?"

"Yeah," she said quickly. "Because if you don't work on Thursday nights—"

Uh-ohhhhhhhhhh . . .

"—I've got an extra ticket—"

Uh-Ohhhhhhhhhh . . .

"—to the Jimmy Fund Benefit tomorrow—"

"What?" I gulped.

"—at the New Blinstrub's."

"The New Blinstrub's? Gee, a lot of our guests want to go there."

"Lots of Red Sox players are going to be at this benefit."

"Red Sox?" I choked.

"Wade Boggs, Roger Clemens. So if you're interested—"

I gulped again before I answered, "*Sure* I'm interested." We'd reached the library now, but I was hoping she wouldn't get out of the car until she told me everything.

"It's at eight tomorrow night."

"What time do you want me to pick you up?"

"At seven?"

"Sure!"

"But there's something else you should know."

"What?"

"It's formal," she said in a no-way-around-it voice. "You're going to have to wear a tuxedo."

"No problem." Dad didn't take his tuxedo when he moved out, and I knew I hadn't grown that much since the junior prom.

"Okay, then." She opened the car door, but didn't move yet. "I gotta go, so I'll come by your homeroom tomorrow before school and give you directions."

I was going to say, "No, that's okay, I'll come by your homeroom," but I caught myself just in time. She was great enough to take me to something like this, I'd risk having people think we were going out.

"Okay!"

"Okay!" she answered, offering me her hand to shake. "Nice to meet you, Bill."

"Nice to meet you, Mary," I said, shaking it firmly. "And thanks! Thanks a lot!"

She got out of the car and shut the door. I didn't

pull away right away because all of a sudden I heard a little kid's voice. "Mary!"

Mary turned, and so did I to see where this kid was. Trouble was, he was too little and didn't even come up to the car window. But I could see his mother walking over and smiling when Mary turned to look at her.

"Hi, Mrs. Sullivan. Oh!" she said, suddenly remembering to be polite, "Mrs. Sullivan, I'd like you to meet my new friend Bill Richards."

I have to admit I was glad she said "new friend" and not "boyfriend." I mean, let's not get carried away here.

"Mary," I heard the little kid say, "are you gonna read—" And then he stopped before he said the name of the book, because he really wanted to get it right: *"The Antelope Who Loved Cantaloupe?"*

Mary laughed. "Of course I will, Matthew!" She turned back to me. "See you tomorrow!" Then she took the kid's left hand as his mother took the other one. Finally I saw him as they walked him up the library steps, every now and then pulling up his arms so that they could glide him above a few stairs, as Mary told him the newest thing that had happened to the Antelope Who Loved Cantaloupe.

I looked at my watch. I had just enough time to get to work. But if I went back to school and told the kids about how it had gone with Mary, I'd be late.

But I headed my car back to school, convincing myself that not too many guests check in till six, anyway, and that John wouldn't squeal on me. I wanted to let the kids know how great Mary was.

But, strangely enough, at the same time I was still feeling lousy because I didn't say yes to her right away when she asked me about Thursday, not until

I'd heard what she wanted me to go to. If she'd said a movie or another trip to the Sizzler, I guess I would have said no.

I drove back to the school, parked in the *teachers'* parking lot, ran up the stairs, and jog-walked to and into the *Dallinews* office.

They were all still there.

They'd been waiting for me.

"Well?"

"Well?"

"Well?"

"Well?"

I nodded slowly and—I could feel it—with total confidence. "She'll be fine. Just fine."

9

The next day I got to school so early *I* could have driven Eddie to work. I was the only person in the whole homeroom.

Until, of all people, Mr. Aronson arrived—because Ms. Cohen, my regular homeroom teacher, was out. So they had to drag in Aronson. And because I was the only kid in the room, he had to go and ask, "Is there a problem, Mr. Richards?" You just can't win. If you're early it's a problem, if you're late, that's a problem, too!

But as it turns out, I saw pretty soon that I did have a problem: Mary wasn't showing up with the directions. I watched every kid come through the room—from Krishna Rahaman to Susan Russell—but with one minute to go before the bell, Mary still hadn't walked in.

Wasn't she going to show? Was she out sick?

Riiinnnggggg!

Now what? Was tonight off? She knew she had to give me directions to her house. Unless she forgot, unless she was sick . . .

Unless she just changed her mind and decided she didn't want to go with me.

If I was going to be really honest about it, it really would have been fair for her to change her mind. After she'd thought about it a while, maybe she figured I didn't deserve to go to a big thing like this. I mean, I didn't say yes until I heard it was an event where Wade Boggs and Roger Clemens would be. So who would blame her? She might be Miss Inner Beauty, but she didn't have to be Miss Wimp.

Uncomfortable as a school-desk chair is, I slunk in the seat and just lay there like a zucchini. And of course that meant it wasn't long before Aronson mentioned me in his list of "Mr. Roche, Miss Rawlings, Mr. Richards, don't you have anything to do?"

So I opened my Physical Science book and stared at it, turning a page every now and then to make it look like I might be reading. I know no one's mind can be a complete blank—everybody's always got to be thinking of something—but my mind was probably thinking as close to nothing as you can get. I didn't even notice when a kid came in with a note.

But then I did hear Aronson say, "Mr. Richards?"

I looked up and saw him holding up an envelope by the edge, like it was contaminated with radioactive dust. "A message from Garcia."

A lot of kids in the room mouthed the words. "A message from Garcia" along with him, because Aronson's always saying "A message from Garcia" —whatever that means—whenever a note arrives for someone. He thinks it's a really hilarious thing to say.

But this time I didn't mind his so-called humor, because I was more interested in the note, which I was hoping was from Mary. Still, even if it was, I sure didn't know what it was going to say.

I didn't even wait to get back to my seat to read it, but opened the envelope, unfolded the letter, and read it right there in front of everyone.

Dear Bill—I had some work I had to do for my term(inal) paper. Here are the directions.

See you at 7 in your tux! As always, Mary.

And she'd written out directions with everything spelled out to the last tenth of a mile. She'd drawn a little map, too, with everything I needed to know to get me to 24 Canal Way in Linden. Good thing—because Linden was a pretty far distance away from Ardmore.

She did want me to go after all.

Mom walked back a few steps and looked at me the way an art critic stares at a painting.

"I think it's a lit-tle big, but it's fine."

"I'm glad it's too big," I told her, "or else I'd feel starched to death." Then I pulled up the cummerbund for the twelfth time in ten minutes. "But I wish this stupid thing was smaller so it wouldn't keep slipping."

"Maybe it'll feel tighter after the meal," she said, before reaching up to give me a kiss on my cheek. "Have a good time, and give the Red Sox my best."

Then she pulled back and smiled, and I got to see once again how pretty Mom is. In fact, she'd be a strong candidate for any *Ms.* Inner or Outer Beauty Contest.

Finally I got to Linden, and finally Canal Way, too. It was a nicer street than the one where I lived. And of course every car on the street was better than mine, too. 24 Canal Way was a huge house. Much bigger than any in Ardmore.

Before I got out of my car, I made sure not to shut off the car radio. Sure, sometimes it made the car even harder to start, but it'd be worth it. This way, after Mary and I had gotten in the car and I'd turned on the ignition, the radio'd start right up and fill the car with songs or talk. Anything to take the heat off us having to think of things to talk about.

Though, I remembered as I approached the doorbell of the big, impressive house, Mary hadn't made it especially hard to talk.

I rang the bell, which wasn't a "Bzzzzt!" like ours, but a chime that played a bunch of notes. And I had a feeling these weren't just a bunch of pretty notes strung together; I got the impression this was the beginning of a famous piece of classical music or an opera or something.

Then the front door—which had the doorknob in the middle of it, for some reason—opened real slow, like it was the door of a bank safe. A little girl, who looked sort of like a five-year-old version of Mary, peeked out from behind it.

"You Bill?"

"Gee-*nah!*" I heard Mary say, though I didn't see her yet. A second later she was there, though, sweeping the kid away, like she wished I hadn't even found out the kid existed.

All I was looking at, though, was Mary's hair. She'd done it really different—high up on her head with a few squiggly-squirly strands hanging down on each side around her ears. I didn't like it.

"Bill, won't you come in?"

"Yeah, sure, thanks," I said, walking in and hearing the stereo playing the type of music they wrote in Vienna hundreds of years ago.

"What do you think of my hair?"

"It's great," I lied. What else could I say?

"Mr. Norman in Copley Square did it," she said in a way that made me think he must be some big-deal beauty-parlor guy. And I guess I wasn't looking too impressed, because she stopped smiling and said, "Come in and meet my mother."

I hate meeting parents almost as much as I hate April's Greek god, but what could I do? Actually, I was pretty grateful she said mother and not parents, and that I'd only have to meet one of them. Unless her father was upstairs and was going to come down in a minute.

We walked through a hallway that could have starred in an Ethan Allen Great Furniture of America commercial. It had a grandfather clock, tall cabinets with glassed-in fronts, and an expensive-looking set of china on its shelves. On the walls were paintings of men from the waist up, guys who looked like they'd fought in the Revolutionary War.

If that wasn't enough, we went into a room that was filled with leather-bound books on shelves built right into the wall. There was even a book stand, the type you see a dictionary sitting on in a real library. But what I noticed was that instead of a dictionary sitting on that book stand, there was an Emily Post Etiquette Book. It wasn't opened up, but it was there, ready in case somebody needed to look up something in a hurry. Holy cow, meeting a mother wasn't pressure-packed enough—but this was someone who kept an etiquette book handy. No wonder her daughter turned out to be Miss Inner Beauty. I'd really have to watch myself!

Mrs. Mulcahy was sitting in a tall, leather-covered chair, reading a book (hardcover, of course). We did the Mother-this-is-Bill-Richards-Bill-this-is-my-mother-how-are-you-it's-nice-to-meet-yous. But all the while this was going on, I noticed that Mrs. Mulcahy seemed like she couldn't move too much. I wasn't sure if she was sick, or if this was the way an etiquette book told you you were supposed to sit.

"I'm sorry you can't meet Mr. Mulcahy," she said, "but he's out of town on business."

"Yeah, I'm sorry, too."

Mary broke out into a big smile. I figured she must have known I was full of it—Miss Inner Beauties aren't necessarily stupid—but I didn't think she'd actually say, "Bill's glad Dad's not here."

"Huh? No—"

"Because," she interrupted in a voice that let me know it was all right and it didn't matter, "Dad's the one who got the tickets, and he's the one who would've taken me tonight if he weren't in Cleveland."

I tried to laugh in a way to show I liked her joke, but I liked it even better when she added, "We'd better get going." I'm much better at the nice-meeting-you-yes-it-was-nice-meeting-*yous* than the mother-this-is-Bill-Richards-Bill-this-is-my-mother-how-are-you-it's-nice-to-meet-yous.

I hadn't even turned the ignition when Mary gushed, "You look really great!"

"Thanks. Uh, you look great, too." And, I thought, as I started the car, aside from her hair, she did. Her purple dress made her look better than the L. L. Bean clothes—a lot better. Though, I thought, it did look like any other dress a girl would wear to any other party. Was it fancy enough for something that was supposed to be formal? To tell the truth, I thought I looked a lot more formal than she did.

"Um," she said, "I do have one request, though."

"Name it," I said, with a single shake of the head, turning off the radio so she could talk and not have to compete with it.

"I'd like to try to write an article about tonight for *Dallinews*."

"Sure," I said. "It sounds like a great idea."

"Well, I figured you might want to do it—"

"Hey," I said, "it's only fair you write it up, since you got the tickets."

"Great. Thanks."

"How many Red Sox players are supposed to be there, anyway?"

"I don't know," she admitted, sounding like she didn't want me to get my hopes too high just in case. "At least a few. You like the Sox?"

"I like every Boston team," I answered. "The Red Sox, Celtics, Bruins, Patriots, and even the Breakers when they were here that year. And if someone starts the National Darts League and we get a team called the Boston Points, I'll like them, too. How about you?" I said a little more softly, letting her know I wasn't going to come down on her too hard if she was like most girls and didn't like sports too much.

And she did make a "tsk" sound to let me know in advance she wasn't going to really agree with me. "I like the Red Sox, Celtics, Bruins, and Patriots, too, but I sort of like all teams."

Though I find talking while driving sometimes as hard as walking and talking—it means I have to take my eye off the road and look at the person—I had to look over after hearing that remark. She smiled, showing me she didn't expect me to understand. "I like it when different teams win," she explained. "When I was a little kid, I saw the Philadelphia

Phillies on TV win the World Series for the very first time in their history. Seeing the parades and the parties on the news made a big impression on me. Everybody was so happy and having such a great time, I thought, this should go on in every city every year so every town'd get a chance to celebrate something. So I root for a different team every year. It's like, you know, sharing."

All right, she didn't sound like your average sports fan, but did this girl have Inner Beauty or what?

"Well," I decided to ask, "do you really like sports, or do you just like watching the celebrations?"

"Oh, no," she laughed. "I love sports, too."

She sounded definite about it, but if there's one thing I've learned, it's this: When a lot of girls say they "love" sports, what they really mean is they'll sit there in front of a game on TV if a guy really wants to see it. True, Mary sounded like she really liked sports so much that she wouldn't understand why everyone didn't (Mary, meet April), but I still wasn't convinced. I'd have to give her Mike's Big Test.

Mike's Big Test is this. He says (and I agree with him) that a girl can really and honestly be considered a sports fan *if she will watch a game on TV when she's all alone in the house*.

"Seen any good games lately?"

I wasn't looking her way, but I could feel her sit up in her seat and turn closer to me. "Yes! Did you see the Ohio State-Michigan basketball game last night on ESPN?"

"Um, no . . ."

And I could feel she was glad to have the chance to fill someone in on the excitement. "Michigan was ahead by 22 at the half, 17 with eleven minutes to go—but Ohio State tied it with four seconds to go! And Michigan's last-minute desperation shot came *this close,*'' she said, squeezing together her thumb and whatever the finger next to it is called, and moving them right in front of my eyes so I wouldn't even have to turn. "Then Ohio State won it at the buzzer. Wow!'' she said, flopping back in her seat as the memories came back in her head. "I wished my father hadn't been away so he could have seen it. He graduated from Ohio State.''

So she hadn't watched it with her father . . . and I didn't think that her mother with the etiquette books or little Gina were right there rooting along beside her. And chances were good Mary wasn't watching it with her boyfriend, because if she had one, he'd be the one driving her to the Jimmy Fund benefit.

Well, then. I couldn't be sure, but I had a feeling that Mary had just gotten an A+ on Mike's Big Test.

We got to the New Blinstrub's and I drove into their lot. My car, of course, was the worst one there, and when the guy they had doing the parking got in to drive it away, he looked at me like he was entering a leper colony.

But however bad I felt about it melted away when we got inside the place. "This is great!'' I said, as we walked along a glassed-in entryway that looked out over the Charles River and a beautifully lit city of Boston.

"Yes, it is nice,'' Mary said in a way that sort of gave me the feeling that this wasn't her first time here. Her parents probably took her to eat here three or four times a year.

We got to the door of the Abigail Adams Suite,

where a woman was taking tickets and giving out little programs. Mary handed me my ticket, and I hoped I'd have a chance to look it over and see how much it cost before I'd have to hand it over to the ticket-taker.

So there I was, walking along, straining my eye downward, trying to see what price was printed on it—

$250! Outrageous! And yet I wasn't too surprised. This was a pretty great place.

I handed the ticket over and got my program—"A sure collectors' item," I told Mary, who nodded real hard in agreement—and we walked inside. One look at the crowd and—

"Wow! Look!"

Sticking out above everybody's heads were three others: Larry Bird's, Kevin McHale's, and Robert Parrish's.

Mary looked at me, real surprised. "I didn't know the Celtics were going to be here, too!"

And as we were staring at these three famous heads, all of a sudden a big, big guy with a drink in each hand squeezed in front of us. "Excuse me!" and slid past us.

I looked at Mary, then pointed at the guy. "That's Craig James!" I said, somehow managing to whisper and scream at the same time. "The guy who just excused himself to us is someone who's been in a Super Bowl!"

But Mary just looked kind of funny, and I pulled back my hand like I'd just stuck it in an electric fan. That's right—you're not supposed to point, are you? And with an etiquette book at home always ready to be looked at, Mary must have thought that guys who point were barbarians.

Or maybe it was something else—that she thought I sounded like too much of a groupie. It's one thing for a girl to go crazy over a football player, but face it, a guy doesn't sound too cool when he's gushing over a 200-pound running back.

But then, no, she gave me a little smile and the funny look went away as quickly as it had come over her. Maybe I was wrong, maybe it had nothing to do with me, maybe it was just that she still wasn't used to seeing famous people, either. "I didn't know the Patriots were going to be here, too," she said.

"Yeah?" I said in a voice that was the highest it'd been since I was 11. "Well, everybody's here."

Everybody was. Here were Roger Clemens and Wade Boggs and Dwight Evans and Bob Stanley, and they even brought out Carl Yastrzemski and Ted Williams for this one. Tony Eason and Irving Fryar were also there from the Patriots, and Rick Middleton and Gord Kluzak were there from the Bruins.

"I hope we get a chance to talk to them," Mary said.

"Yeah. I'd love to ask Clemens how it feels to know you struck out more guys in one game than any pitcher ever did."

She nodded. "And I'd like to ask Larry Bird how he can make the adjustment to playing on the regular floor at, say, Madison Square Garden on Friday after he's played on the parquet floor in Boston Garden on Thursday."

Never mind Mike's Big Test—I'd just learned that Mary not only liked sports, she really knew them, too. Any fan could have asked my question, but here was one that was really interesting.

But neither one of us got to ask any questions,

because a few seconds later there was an announcement that we all had to go to our tables, and the stars were at the long straight one at the front of the room while we were at an ordinary round one where there was nobody famous—just a bunch of husbands and their wives (who weren't dressed any fancier than Mary, I noticed). For a while these people seemed to get a kick out of the fact that two kids were at the table. They asked us who we liked in sports and—of course—what grades we were in. Then they left us alone.

Still, it was great to be there and hear Red Sox announcer Alan Hutchings make some good jokes, introduce everybody, and hear their good jokes, too.

There was one problem, though: the food. There wasn't much of it, and sure not enough for $250. But I wasn't going to be like April at my cousin's wedding. I just quietly ate the miniature piece of meat with the miniature piece of broccoli after I polished off the miniature salad and the miniature roll, which even had only a miniature pad of butter. And after everything I was still so hungry I considered eating the other miniature pad of butter all by itself. But I wouldn't complain.

But I was sure surprised when Mary leaned her head over, moved it right next to mine, and whispered through clenched teeth, "You could starve here, you know that?"

I had to laugh before I could answer, "Sure could."

"And for what these tickets cost, they should have an all-you-can-eat buffet."

I laughed at that too, but I knew some of the laughter came because I just felt relieved. It was great that Mary could criticize the food when she was responsible for us being there—unlike April. I almost told her right then and there how great she was.

*   *   *

"And second-to-last, but not least," said Alan Hutchings, "we'd like to pay special tribute to a man Boston will always remember. I was announcing that Patriots game when 42 seconds and 13 points separated them from defeat. I was wrapping up, saying, 'Our technical director is Don Baker, our engineer is Al Walker,' and 42 seconds later I was screaming along with everyone else . . ."

"The way we screamed about Doug Flutie that November day in 1984," I whispered to Mary, who didn't say anything . . . who was looking kind of funny again . . .

Then Alan Hutchings started talking again, so I took the chance to look back at him. "We hear a lot about the Outrageous Onside Kick," he was saying, referring to Boston's most recent legendary sports achievement. "But let's never forget the man who ran 72 and 82 yards from scrimmage on those third downs—Mr. Craig James!"

First the first row, then the second, then all of us were up and giving Craig James a Standing O. But out of the corner of my eye I saw Mary get up a little slower than the rest of us. And she wasn't clapping hard, either. In fact, she even looked like she wanted to cry.

Wow. What happened? I could see, too, that she wasn't about to break into the type of crying people do when they're happy someone's won an award. Mary was almost-crying about something different, something else entirely.

I didn't know what it was, so I must have looked really confused. Mary could see it, too. And I guess it got her nervous. She grabbed her little purse and pushed her chair back.

"Excuse me—"

She turned around and walked out fast, so fast that a few of the people at the table stopped watching Craig James go to the mike and looked at this girl running away. Then they all looked at me. I semi-smiled, trying to give them the impression that Mary did stuff like this all the time, but they just kept looking at me like I must have said something dirty to her or something. On one guy's face was a look that said, "This is what happens when you invite kids to a big fancy party like this."

Never mind about that—something was wrong, and I had to go after Mary and find out what it was. I left and just stormed out the same direction she'd gone.

But once I got outside the door to the hall I didn't see her. And I didn't know what to do. Had she gone to the ladies' room?

I decided to find it and wait outside it for her, just for a minute or two, in case she was in there. A waiter passed by me, so I said, "Excuse me, sir!" realizing just in time I'd better not tap on his right shoulder because it might make him drop the tray he had on his left one. "Where's the ladies' room?"

Not until I said it did I hear how weird that sounded. And the waiter didn't make it easier—he looked at me like I was a pervert. "The *ladies'* room?"

"Never mind." All of a sudden I didn't need to know, anyway—because I could see Mary through the glass-wall entrance, standing outside where the cabs drive up. I didn't know what she was doing there, but I rushed to the door and went outside to find out.

As I came over to her from behind, though, I could see her wince. Obviously she'd seen me coming out of the corner of her eye.

And I could see that she'd been crying.

"I'm sorry . . ." she began.

"No, come on, it's okay."

I wanted her to know, too, that I wasn't going to make her explain. Times like these are like accidents; they're times to be quiet.

She started to talk, though, and surprised me with what she said. "If I knew Craig James was going to be here," she shrugged, "I wouldn't have come."

Craig James? I wanted to say. Now I was really confused. But that wasn't important. I just decided to ask, "Do you want to leave?"

She tried to smile, shrug, and make a joke. "Well, there was only one more award left, anyway . . ."

I nodded. "I'll have them get the car."

She reached out to stop me and her face got a little serious. "You mind?"

"No! Course not!" And I really didn't. We'd gotten to see most everything, and I was grateful for what I had seen and wouldn't get mad about what I'd miss.

But after I gave the garage guy the ticket for the car and stood there waiting, I kept thinking, *How can Craig James be the reason Mary's crying?* I wasn't ready to believe she was his girlfriend and that *they'd* just broken up.

I turned and looked at Mary, and recognized what the look on her face said: The pain she was feeling was the type you feel when someone you love doesn't love you anymore.

Still, all the time we waited, I didn't bring anything like that up. And even without saying a word, I think she could feel that I was saying to her, "Handle it the way you want to."

And so we stayed quiet for a pretty long time. It

wasn't the type of quiet Mom and Dad used to have after they had a fight and nobody was speaking to anybody. I was pretty sure that Mary knew the quiet I was giving her meant that I was on her side.

At least that's what I felt right then. By the time they brought the car to us, I have to admit, I was starting to go crazy out of curiosity. I almost blew it and turned around and asked her, "What's wrong?" But I didn't.

After the first few minutes in the car, though, I wished I'd done my old trick and turned the radio on before we'd parked it. We sure could have used it.

That's when I started worrying that maybe Mary didn't know I understood. The closer we got to her house, the more I wondered if she was thinking I wasn't talking to her because I was mad at her. Maybe it'd be better to say something to let her know I didn't hate her.

But the thing to do was to talk about something safe. Maybe ask her if she wanted to go someplace and eat. No, I decided, that's no good. When you're crying, you don't feel like eating, even if you were starving the moment before you thought about the person who started you crying.

But I couldn't think of anything better, and we were getting closer and closer to her house.

"Would you like to go someplace and get something to eat? Like you said, we sure didn't get a lot of food at dinner."

She smiled at my little joke. "No. No, thanks."

"Okay."

"Unless *you* want to."

"No, no, that's okay, it's cool."

More silence, where I tried to think of something. But just as I was about to turn on the radio, she said, "You must think I'm crazy."

"No, Mary, I don't."

"My boyfriend Jim and I," she started, "were at Sullivan Stadium the day Craig James got those two touchdowns."

"Oh . . ."

"We were in the first row of the end zone where he scored them, and he looked right at us both times after he rushed in . . ."

I didn't know what to say. "Wow"? "Gee"? I just kept quiet, and she went on: "It was like an omen. After the game, I felt closer to Jim than I'd ever felt to any other person in my life." She made a sad sound. "Until a few months later, I found out he was dating another girl all the time he was dating me."

Like all my friends who'd listened to my awful story, I didn't know what else to say besides "I'm sorry." Then Mary got quiet again, and even though we were just a few streets from her house now, I decided to ask, "Want me to turn on the radio?"

"Yeah," she said, "just as long as they're not playing a country song like . . . 'I'm So Blue over You I Might Do Anything.' "

I laughed—I think she wanted me to—and then she laughed, too. And I turned on the radio, which was playing Iron Maiden's "Stranger in the Strange Land," which, thank God, has nothing to do with being in love or having someone fall out of love with you.

When we got to her house, she opened her little purse and wriggled out a folded-up program. "Here. I made you leave so fast, you didn't even get to take yours."

Usually I would have said, "No, that's okay." But I knew she'd only say, "No, take it!" and then

I'd say, "No, it's okay" again. And neither one of us felt like going through that.

And there was another thing: I knew that she was "paying me back" because I'd listened to her problems, the way I used to buy meals at McDonald's and tickets to the movies whenever a friend would listen to me about April. None of them back then could ever convince me that they didn't mind, and I'd never be able to convince Mary, either. So I took the program. Then I put my hand on her shoulder and kept it there for a few seconds. Maybe it was the time for a kiss, but . . .

"Thanks," she said.

I shook my head no. "Thank *you*. Really."

But somehow saying that even hurt her more. "G'night," she said feebly, then opened the door, got out quick, and closed it. Forget her mother's etiquette book—I knew she didn't want me to walk her to her house.

Mom looked surprised when I walked in.

"Bill! Home so early?"

"Yeah, it wasn't long."

"Was it good?" she asked, amazed I hadn't brought that part of it up as soon as I walked in the door.

I'd have to get back the excitement I had before Mary got upset. "Yeah, great time. Some of the Celtics and the Patriots were there, too."

"Oh, good," she said, glad for me, even though sports teams don't mean anything to her. "How did Mary look?"

"Um, good."

"What did she wear?"

Usually I would have said, "Something purple, I don't know," but I figured if I talked about clothes, I wouldn't have to talk about what had just happened. "She was wearing a purple dress that didn't look too fancy. None of the women were wearing what I thought were fancy dresses. How come?"

Mom was smiling because she enjoys when she can teach me something. "Well," she laughed. "If you expected to see women in hoopskirts, they stopped wearing them after the Civil War."

"No, I didn't expect something like that, but I did expect something else."

"What?"

I thought about it, but all I could do was shrug. "I don't know."

"No," she smiled, coming over and readjusting my bow tie. "A woman only has to wear a very nice dress at a formal function. We have it a lot easier than you men."

If it had been five hours earlier, I might have said something about how women *always* have it a lot easier than guys. But after what I'd seen Mary feeling about losing someone she loved, and what I remembered feeling over April, I wasn't as sure about that anymore.

10

I've heard Mom say that the problem when people invite you to their house—and you go—is that then you have to invite them over your house—and they come. Now I knew what she meant.

The next day I thought a lot about calling Mary to ask her out, considering she'd asked me out. Or at least calling her to see how she was doing.

Well, Mom always did invite those people who'd invited her back over to our place. I guess that meant I really had to ask Mary out to pay her back.

I stopped by Eddie's after school to get her phone number. He didn't make it easy, and didn't even try to keep in his Santa smile when he said, "You like her?"

I swatted the line away the way a defensive line-backer bats away an on-target pass. "Ed, come on, she asked me out to something terrific. It'd be lousy not to ask her out to thank her."

"Well, you don't really have to," he said, still smiling.

Of course I knew what he wanted—for me to say that I liked her. Instead, I let out a big breath. "I don't really need this, Ed."

But he pretended he was innocent. "What do you mean?"

"Ed—"

"Ahhhhm sorry," he said, putting his arm around my neck and doing what I think they call "scruffing it." "I'm just glad to see you getting over April."

"I'm not getting over April. Well, I mean, I am, but that doesn't mean I'm going to get into anything with Mary."

He answered that by picking up a doughnut. "Grape jelly," he said. And he didn't make it sound like he was offering the doughnut to me, but said it in a way to let me know he thought my answer was bull.

I pointed at him. (I didn't have to worry about etiquette with Ed.) "Whatever you do, don't you go telling her I wanted her number."

Well, that made him give out with a big, bellowy "Ho-ho-ho."

"I mean it, Ed. If you two are riding back and forth all the way in from Linden every day, you've always got to be looking for things to talk about. Hey," I said, right as it was occurring to me, "Did Mary say anything about me today on the way in?"

Well, for some reason Ed thought that was a riot, too. He arched his back and just roared.

"All right," I snarled, "don't tell me."

Now his eyes actually twinkled like Santa Claus's. "Bill, I could be wrong, but I think she's going to figure out you wanted her number when you call her."

That started the ho-ho-ho's again, and who could blame him? I hadn't realized that, yeah, of course she'd know I'd went after her number if I was there on the phone talking to her. It even made me laugh too for a second, before I got off my stool to leave.

"And I'm leaving without having a doughnut," I told him. "Not because I'm mad you're right. I'm starting to get too out of shape coming here so much. Black coffee and more trips to the gym, that's what I need."

Somehow I had a feeling Ed was going to say something like, "Gotta look good for Mary, huh?" or at least smile to let me know he was thinking it. But he didn't. He just said, "369-1379," and let the rest of it drop.

Still, I waited a day before I called her. And even when I'd made up my mind, I tried stalling it as long as I could. I paced on the kitchen floor, moving like a knight in chess, walking two tile squares forward, one to the left, two squares forward, one to the right, two to the left, one up, two to the right, one down . . .

Because I still didn't know what I was going to ask her out to. A basketball or hockey game seemed like a natural, but would being at a game remind her of her boyfriend? A movie? It seemed too cheap after what she'd taken me to. Going out to dinner? That might seem too much like a date, instead of the I'm-just-paying-you-back type of night this was going to be.

Still, the more I thought about it, the better going out to dinner seemed, because dinner is what she'd taken me out to. Only thing was, now I had to think of a restaurant to take her to.

I used to take April to The Captain of the Guard, the restaurant in our hotel. In the days when April and I used to come into The Captain once a week, we got treated like we were little celebrities, a lot better, I can tell you, than we would have been treated at any other restaurant, because everybody at the hotel knew me. Ms. Algarotti used to come by and say hello, and Mr. Underwood, one of the regulars, would sometimes send us over free desserts.

So everybody there got real used to seeing me with April, and it was pretty embarrassing when I had to tell Ms. Algarotti and Mr. Underwood and everybody else what happened. People I didn't tell—people like John, Stan, and Rana—eventually asked me things like, "Hey, where's that pretty girl you've been seeing?" and I'd have to tell them that I wasn't seeing her anymore, that we broke up. Yeah, *we!* Like I'd had a lot to do with the decision.

All right, I thought, grabbing the phone, that's enough about April. Just take Mary out to dinner someplace else, but call!

I started pushing buttons fast, pushed one wrong one, and had to start over. That's because I'd been thinking how everyone at work had said they were sorry in the best way they could, and told me they hoped I'd get a new girlfriend fast. I couldn't bring Mary in, since she wasn't my girlfriend and wasn't going to be. No way was I ready for another girlfriend.

And another thing was for sure—I was going to take Mary somewhere where there'd be no chance any of the guys would see us. I mean, we all promised that we wouldn't get tangled up with girls ever again, and I wasn't going to be the first one to break that promise.

Anyway, this time I pressed all seven buttons right (what an achievement!). There with the phone next to my ear, I heard the thing hadn't started ringing yet. Well, I thought, I still have a chance to hang up.

No. I had to go through with it.

Burrrrrrrrrrrr.

Mary's telephone was one of those high-class suburban phones that don't really ring—they just make very soft *Burrrrrrrrrrrrr*s.

Burrrrrrrrrrrr.

It was almost like ringing was too low-class a thing for a phone to do. Maybe Mary's mother found something in the etiquette book on how a telephone should sound and told the telephone man that—

"Hel-*LO-O-O!*"

Ever notice how in a house with little kids, it's the little kid who loves to answer the phone? "Hi, Gina."

"Hiiii! Whodis?"

"Mary's friend Bill Richards."

"Marrr-reeeeeeeeee!" And then there was a *thunk* as she dropped the phone on the floor.

First time I ever called April and her mother answered, she asked who I was, and I made the mistake of just saying, "A friend." She got awfully suspicious, and, in all the time I dated April, her mother never really got over it and always looked at me real suspiciously. That's when I learned it's better to tell the person who answers the phone—even if it's a little kid—your name and everything else they want to know. You might need that person to trust you and like you someday.

Though Gina was in another room now, I could hear her still yelling "Marrr-reeeeeeeeee!" Then I could hear some female voices saying something, but I couldn't make out what it was, with the classical music playing in the background. Oh, well—at least it told me that they weren't just playing the stuff when I was there to make me think they were a cultured family. But I guess I should have realized that Miss Inner Beauty's family wouldn't pretend to be anything they really weren't—

"Hello?"
"Mary?"
"Bill!" She laughed nervously. "Are you calling to see if they took me away to the Funny Farm?"
"No." It hadn't occurred to me that she might be embarrassed about two nights ago, though I could see why she would be. But I just plowed ahead and asked, "I was calling to see if you wanted to go to dinner next week?"
Silence for a second. Hey, what did I do wrong? I never thought she'd say no.
But she wasn't saying no yet, not exactly. "Are you asking me because you feel sorry—ummmmmmm, never mind, *yes,* it'd really be great to go out to dinner. Really great."

11

On our way to the restaurant, I thought it'd be a good idea if we talked about everything else but what had happened at the Jimmy Fund banquet. Not that we couldn't talk about sports:

"I can't believe the slump Danny Ainge is in."

"Yes," she agreed, "but I don't think he deserves to be booed, not after all he's done for the Celtics."

"Yeah. Isn't it amazing how fans'll boo a guy to death—and then as soon as he scores a three-pointer—"

"—they cheer! But can you imagine what getting booed by thousands of people must be like? I'd die if somebody booed me. Imagine at the library if someone asked me for a book and I had to say it was out—"

"—and all the people sitting in the library booed you?"

"Yes!" she said, then laughed. "And can you imagine what'd happen if everybody in the lobby booed you when you couldn't give someone a room?"

"Actually," I answered, "it'd be better than picking up broken cigarette-machine parts."

"Still," she smiled, "people shouldn't boo players when they do something wrong, especially when they've seen them do something great and'll probably see them do something great again real soon."

It was talk like that that reminded me I was talking to Miss Inner Beauty.

After we finally arrived in the North End and found a parking place (it's not easy), we talked about work while walking to the restaurant. Somehow, this time I didn't have as much of a problem walking and talking and looking at her and where I was walking at the same time.

"My boss is great," she told me. "He never makes anything seem like a big deal."

"My boss *was* great. She's getting transferred to the Quality Court in New York."

"Oh. You nervous about it?"

I liked that she was smart enough to realize it could mean trouble. "A little." I nodded. "Like my grandmother used to say, 'The devil you know—' "

She finished it with me. " '—is better than the devil you don't know.' " There may be a big difference between my house and Canal Way, but maybe our grandmothers were alike.

"Yeah, her last day's the day after tomorrow. We all chipped in for a gift. We're having a party for her."

Then I stopped. I'd better shut up, I thought, or she'll think I'm going to ask her to the party. And then I'd have to.

But I was in luck. Mary was thinking of something else instead. "Were you in on the buying of the gift?"

"No."

"I hope whoever did the buying," she said, "didn't buy a joke gift. I don't think that's ever a good idea. It really makes it seem like you don't care too much."

While I was thinking that yeah, she really is Miss Inner Beauty, I saw her walk a few steps out of her way to get to a guy who was giving out pamphlets. The way she walked so fast and with so much, I don't know, determination, I wondered how she knew even before she got to him that she wanted one of his pamphlets so bad. Had she seen him before and meant to get one then, or did she lose the one she got before? Was this a real valuable coupon or something? Should I be getting one, too?

And what confused me even more was that as soon as we got to the next trash can on the street, she crumpled up the pamphlet she just got and dropped it in there.

I guess she could tell from the look on my face I was pretty surprised, so I told her why. "Gee, you went out of your way to get the thing, and did you even look at it?"

She shook her head in a no-you-don't-understand way. "These guys get paid by how many they give out," she explained. "So I like to take them from them, even if I'm not really interested in what they're selling."

Miss Inner Beauty.

After we got seated in Francesca's, we talked about the movies we'd just seen on TV:

"*North by Northwest?*" she mentioned.

"Oh, yeah, that one's real good. I'd really like to go to Mount Rushmore some day! You ever see *Psycho*—the first *Psycho,* I mean?"

"Oh, yeah, that one's great, too. I've seen it three times, but every time Norman's mother turns around in her chair, *I* have to turn around. *Bambi?*"

"*Bambi?*"

"Yeah," she said. "*Bambi*. Great movie. I rent it

for my library kids a lot. Though after we finish it I usually have to stay a little late with the kids and stop them from crying."

Miss Inner Beauty. I could also see she was the type of girl who'd like *Give Her the Moon,* but I wasn't going to bring that up.

After dinner, we walked around the Quincy Market and talked about some more ideas she had for the paper:

"How about a column called 'The Best around Dallin'?"

"Hmmmmm . . . 'The Best around Dallin' . . ."

"The Best Pizza Place. Where you can find the Best Video Jukebox. The Best Bowling Alley."

We both said the next one together: "The Best Doughnut Shop."

She smiled. "What do you think?"

"It's good! Write it up and hand it in!"

To make a long story short, we had a really good time. Finally, though, it was over, and we were already in front of her house, with the car still running, partly to keep the heat on, partly so I could have an excuse if I needed one to make a fast getaway. I didn't, though, not even when things got a little serious.

"I'm sorry about the other night."

"Oh, that's okay, really, forget it."

"It's the last time I'm ever going cry over him. And I mean it."

"No, don't apologize, I understand." And then, maybe because she didn't know what else to say, maybe because she wasn't saying anything, I added, "It's happened to me, too."

She turned and looked at me, kind of surprised. I

sort of wished I hadn't brought this up, but now that I had, I guess I'd have to explain.

And so I unbuttoned my coat and told her about my Love at First Sight and Hampton Beach and Ongonquit and even *Give Her the Moon*. Mary sat and listened and looked sad, and, like everybody at the hotel, she made all the right sounds that told me how bad she felt for me.

"So I do understand," I finished. "First you swear to yourself you're not going to bother people by talking about it, and two seconds later you're talking about it."

She nodded. "The only way you can keep from talking about it is when you can manage to get your mind off the person one hundred percent."

"Right," I agreed. "If you can keep the person out of your head. But once she—"

"—or he—"

"—or he comes in your head, that's it, it's over. You're just going to tell the person you're with about her—or him—for the whole rest of the night."

She moved around in her seat a little to get comfortable. "I think that's because you're hoping the person listening to the story is going to come up with something you didn't think of before—"

"Something that's going to make the person you love love you again."

"Yeah."

"Yeah," I echoed, before letting a breath of disgust go through my head. "Only trouble is, they never do."

She laughed weakly. "Never. They try hard, and they say they're sorry—"

"They *are* sorry."

"Oh, I know they are! And then," she said softly,

"you're sorry that they're sorry, and sorry you brought it up, because even though you weren't happy or anything, you were both having an okay time up to then."

"The best time you've had since before you lost the person you cared about."

I got a little nervous then. Maybe she thought I was saying I'd been having a good time with her. And while I was, I sure wasn't going to return to Girlfriend Land, so I didn't want her to think that.

But saying nothing made a silence that looked like it was going to go on forever. I decided I could go one of two ways—to more serious talk, or back to the jokes. I decided on the jokes. "Well, I'm just glad I'm getting through the story faster every time I tell it."

And the joke did make her laugh. "Sometimes I tell it so fast I'm sorry when it's over."

"Because then you don't have anything else to talk about the whole rest of the night?"

"Right," she agreed. "But maybe," she said slowly, like she was thinking this for the first time and wasn't sure how it was going to sound, "maybe it means it's not bothering us as much anymore."

I looked at her. "Maybe," I said, though I wasn't convinced of it. (To be fair, I wasn't *not* convinced, either.) "Hey, let me ask you something? Is it too hot in here?"

She widened her eyes and nodded. "Boiling."

I shut off the heat, then the car. I had a feeling I was going to be there a while longer anyway.

"But you know," she added, "in a way April and Jim didn't do anything wrong."

"There," I said flatly to Miss Inner Beauty, "I don't agree with you."

"No," she insisted softly, "it's true."

"I don't know about you, but she was wearing my ring."

"And I was wearing his. But what does that mean? Have you seen those posters that say, 'If you love someone, set him free. If he returns, he is yours; if he doesn't, he never was.'?"

"There's a T-shirt I like better."

And before I could tell her what it was, she gave me a big grin. "The one that says, 'If he doesn't come back, hunt him down and shoot him'?"

The thought of Miss Inner Beauty saying something like that cracked me up. And me cracking up—with my real strange laugh that sounds like a seal barking—cracked her up.

"Yeah," I went on, "there are times I love April like crazy, and they're usually followed by times I want her hit by a truck."

She laughed at that, too. "I know! I understand! I've prayed for a couple of runaway trucks every now and then."

"Or maybe a snowplow!"

"Or a twenty-foot long trailer truck!"

"Or one of those trailers that carry new cars on them!"

Finally, after the laughing died down, I buttoned my coat (all of a sudden it was cold again), and said, "Well, I guess if she doesn't want me, she isn't worth having."

"That's right," Mary agreed.

"Only thing is . . ."

". . . yeah."

Oh, just say it. "I wish I was always as brave as I'm making myself sound now."

"I know," she sympathized.

That's when I thought I saw her hand moving over, like she was going to put it on mine to make me feel better. When I saw it coming, I think I almost jumped, or even did jump a little. But then I relaxed when I saw she was just moving her hand up to her hair so she could fix it a little.

Only question now was, had she been going to put her hand on mine, but decided she'd just better pretend she was fixing her hair when she saw me jump?

Never mind, just say something quick. "Gee, if you turn off the heat, it gets cold right away, doesn't it?"

"Freezing."

But before I could reach over to turn the heat back on, I found that Mary had taken my line as a signal that the night was over. "Well," she said, "I guess I'd better be going." She opened the car door. "Thanks for a nice time."

"Oh, uh—you're welcome."

But then, just before she got out, she looked at me and said, "Maybe we can help each other."

"What?"

She shut the door. "Did you ever hear how in Alcoholics Anonymous the people in it call a friend if they feel like they're going to break down and have a drink?"

"Yeah?"

"Why don't we call each other whenever we're feeling bad about April or Jim?"

"Um—"

"And whoever is feeling bad can be helped by the person feeling good. She—or he—can bring up sports or ideas for the paper or anything else that pops in our heads, anything to just keep us from thinking about April or Jim."

But she'd heard my "Um," and she couldn't pretend she hadn't. "No?"

"Oh, no-no-no?" I said. "It's a great idea."

"Okay, good! What's your number?"

"648-1791."

"And you know mine."

"Yeah."

"369-1379."

"Right."

"Good." Then she opened the door again. But before she got out of the car, she did it—she put her hand on mine. "And Bill?"

"Y-yeah?"

"Next time we go out, let's talk about us, not them."

And to make matters worse (not that I really mean worse), she leaned over, kissed me quick on the cheek, and ran up her walk.

Meanwhile, I was wondering how did she know there was going to be a next time? I didn't.

Or did I?

12

Dallinews doesn't come out till last period, because our principal worries that if it's sold during school hours, the kids'll read it at their desks instead of listening to the teachers, which they probably would.

Course, all of us on the staff love walking down the hall after school on the days the paper comes out. Sure, most kids are talking about something else entirely, but we see a lot of kids leaning against their lockers reading the paper—and sometimes they even tell us how much they like it.

This time walking down the hall, I heard stuff like, "She gets up that early to drive him in every day?" and "Who's Mary Mulcahy?" in between "My mother wouldn't even let me try the boots on," and "I'm moving to California as soon as I graduate from this stupid place." More kids than usual had the paper open to the centerfold (whoops—"editorial well," as Mike calls it), where the Miss Inner Beauty letters were printed.

Meanwhile, I couldn't wait to hear what Mary was going to say when she saw herself nominated.

I didn't have to wait long.

It was when I went walking up Hemlock Street to get my car that I could see someone was leaning against the side door—Mary.

Like I said, I couldn't wait to hear what she had to say, so I walked fast as I could without making it look real obvious. When I got close, though, it looked to me for a second like she was mad about something. No, I decided—she was just kind of emotional from the whole thing and didn't know how to start saying thanks.

So I'd start. I reached down, unlocked the passenger door, and opened it for her. "Need a ride to the library?"

"Bill," she said in a nasty voice, "did you write that letter?"

She wasn't emotional—she was mad! How could she be? I motioned to the car. "You want to get in and we'll talk about it?"

Well, she got in the car, but before I got a chance to close the door, she sure gave me a dirty look. "I'm not going to be in that contest. Take my name off the list." Then she reached over, grabbed the inside handle, and slammed the door shut.

I was so surprised I couldn't even answer. Instead I just walked around to my side half in a daze. What did I do that could've been so wrong?

Anyway, I opened my door and got in. I could see she was still mad, though she'd calmed down a little. I still didn't say anything, though, but just jiggled the key in the ignition, started the engine, and began to drive away.

For a few seconds we didn't talk. If I knew she was going to show up mad, I thought, I might've left the radio on.

But finally she spoke up. "Bill," she said more

softly, "look, I'm sorry, but I want you to take my name off the list."

I still couldn't understand it. 'Wait a minute, Mary—why?"

She looked ahead and let out a long, slow breath, like I was making it harder for her than it had to be. "Never mind why. Just do it, okay?"

"No reason's not enough of a reason," I said, the way I do with Mom when she tries to get me to do things that don't make sense and doesn't give me a reason.

"Okay, you want to know why? Because I'd never be able to get up in front of all those people."

"Wait a minute," I said slowly. "What happened to the kid who was going to be Providence's best anchorwoman?"

Well, it took her a second to come up with an answer to that, and when she did, it wasn't a good one: "Do you know how many people are watching you when you're doing the news?"

"One or two million?"

"I mean in the studio," she answered, annoyed I hadn't gotten what she meant. "Like seven or eight, that's how many watch you. It's different than being up in front of the whole school."

It still seemed like a pretty flimsy argument to me. "All right. But getting to be an anchorwoman in Providence isn't going to be easy. Here's your chance to get on TV and show everybody you got what it takes—"

"No, Bill, come on."

"—so instead of arguing with me," I said louder so she wouldn't be able to stop me, "you should be thinking about what your acceptance speech is going to be so Gerri Jontry on *Local Focals* gets real impressed and can recommend you for a job someday."

"Urrrgh!" she said, like she wanted to strangle me. "Bill, just take my name off the list, will you?!"

The whole thing made me brake a little too hard at the light. "No, wait a minute, come on, Mary, why? Don't you want people to know about this really great thing you're doing?"

"I'm not doing a 'really great thing.' "

"Yes, you are. Getting up at five-thirty five days a week to get Eddie in, in time to open?"

"I'm a morning person," she explained. "I don't mind getting up—"

"I'll bet there's been at least one day when you felt like staying in bed—or even staying home because you were sick—and you went to school just because Eddie wouldn't have gotten in without you."

I thought it was a pretty right thing to say, but all the time I was talking she was shaking her head from side to side. She'd wait for me to finish, but she was letting me know no matter how much I talked, she wasn't going to agree with me. And once I was done talking, she said, "Getting in early before school gives me more time to study. Do you know what my grades are this year compared to last year?"

Now I was the one shaking my head from side to side, letting her talk as much as she wanted and waiting for her to finish, but letting her know I'd never agree with her, either. "The more you tell me what you're doing is no big deal, the more sure I am of something: No offense to Jennifer Fifer, Lora Sobolow, or Joan Ronan, but you really are Miss Inner Beauty."

And that made her explode. "Who wants to be known as the *nicest* kid in school?!"

I was busy turning into the library parking lot, but I still was able to yell, "What's wrong with being nice?!"

"*Plenty,*" she answered. "I was nice to Jim, and look what happened! My girlfriends warned me about taking you to the Jimmy Fund benefit—'Mary, you're being too nice too soon!' they said. And maybe they were right, because what it's done is let you want to tell the world I'm *nice!*"

And even though I hadn't come to a complete stop yet, she wasn't going to wait for me to say anything. She opened the door and got out the moment she could. "Don't you go around telling people I'm nice!"

She was starting to close the door, then she decided to—

Slam!!

And in case I didn't get the message, she bent down, picked up a clump of snow, and threw it on the car. Then she marched up the library steps and into the building. She slammed that door, too.

I'll never understand girls as long as I live.

13

The next morning I kept hoping all the way to the *Dallinews* office that Mary'd be there waiting to tell me she'd thought it over and changed her mind. She'd be in the contest after all.

And as I opened the fire door and looked down the hall, there was a girl waiting for me. Even from far away, I could tell right away who it was.

It wasn't Mary. It was April.

Did she want me back?

Getting closer, I saw for the millionth time just how beautiful she was . . . in a sun-yellow dress that girls usually only wear when it's spring or summer. But the way April looked, it was always spring or summer. There was that wonderful, long, straw-colored hair again, perfectly cut, just reaching the back of her waist . . . I didn't want to, but I automatically remembered about what it was like to put my fingers through that hair . . .

Was she going to apologize? Did she realize what a jerk she'd been? And (I was surprised to find myself thinking) what would I tell Mary if April did apologize and want me back?

But as I got near her, I could see from the look on

her face (and the hands on her hips) that apologizing was the farthest thing from her mind.

Still, maybe if I said "Hi" in a nice way . . .

"Hi."

It was weird to be talking with her this close again.

She didn't say hi back. Instead, just, "Bill, what are you trying to do with this Miss Inner Beauty thing—embarrass Larah?"

"What?"

She brushed back her hair with her black-nailed hand. "Everyone in the whole school knows this contest is just to make it look like what Larah won doesn't mean much. Well, Larah's my friend, and I don't like seeing her treated like that."

Here was the girl I used to talk to all the time—but the talk was never like this. "April, that wasn't why we did it."

She folded her arms. "Okay, so why did you? Whose idea was it, anyway?"

"Well . . . it was mine."

"O-o!" she said sarcastically.

"But I did it because I thought it was time to do something for kids who do nice things—"

"Nice things!" she said sarcastically. "Well, that's because you have a lot of Inner Beauty yourself—right, 'Mr. Inner Beauty?' 'Mr. Wonderful!' Why don't we just have a contest and name you god of the school!"

She whirled around and started to walk away. Then she turned back. "And another thing—that *Give Her the Moon* movie? It absolutely *stunk.*" Then she walked away for good.

But I wouldn't let her. Sure, I felt like my head was swimming, no drowning, but as long as I hadn't gone down for the third time, there was still time for me to do something.

I grabbed her black-nailed hand, and, without being too rough, pulled her around. "Look, April—these days I'm into kids who are nice to people and do the right things—which is why," I said, the words ringing in my ears, but sounding absolutely right, "I wouldn't take you back now even if you wanted to come back."

Her eyes flashed with hate, and she yanked her hand out of mine. "And who wants you back?"

It didn't hurt a bit. She could see I meant what I said and I'd stand by it. My eyes were saying, "Goodbye forever," and she walked away with a lot less determination than she started to before I'd said my piece.

Still, after it was over, I was almost shaking. I thought about Mary's system where we'd call each other if we needed to. I would have loved to have talked to her then, except that Mary wasn't so thrilled about me these days, either.

So I sighed a big one and went into the office. They were all there—Mike, Karen, Luke, and Doug—and they were all applauding.

"Yay!"

"Aw'right!"

"Terrific!"

"That's telling her!"

I looked at them through half-closed eyes. "They don't make the doors in schools too thick these days, do they?"

"Never mind!" Luke yelled. "Guess what! A reporter's coming from *USA Today* to write up the contest!"

"And," Karen excitedly added, "we're getting a

proclamation from Mayor Kinsman that'll make that Friday 'Inner Beauty Day' in Ardmore!"

"Yeah," Doug joked. "After we get the President to declare a National Inner Beauty Day we're going to hit the UN."

"Never mind," Mike said. "It's great, everything's great!"

Not when you know that your front-runner isn't going to run in the race, I thought, as I stood there looking miserable. And I looked miserable long enough for all of them to huddle around me.

"Bill, is this about April?"

"No, she's just a jerk."

"Total jerk."

"But that's not it," I said.

"What is it, then?"

"Yeah, what?"

"What?"

How could I tell them? Just do it fast, I guess. "Mary doesn't want to be in the contest."

"What?"

"What?"

"WHAT?!"

I shrugged. "She's too shy."

"Too shy? I thought you said she wasn't."

"She wasn't," I explained, sitting down and slumping in the chair I always forget is broken, which meant I had to straighten up real fast. "Now she says she is." I was too dazed from my meeting with April to explain to them that Mary didn't want to be known as the nicest kid in school.

They all looked at each other. Then they rushed over to the chair and almost knelt at my feet (and almost knocked me over again).

"Tell her she's got to do it!"

"You can convince her!"

"Work on her!"

"Let her know about what great publicity this'll be for the school, the town—"

"—and all the other girls with Inner Beauty—"

"Promise her anything, but get her to do it!"

Oh, Goddddddddddd! I wanted to scream. But they saw it in my face, and they decided to give me a break.

"Wait a minute," Luke said. "Let's one of us talk to Mary."

"Yeah, that's right," Mike agreed. "Why should Bill always have to do everything?"

"Don't flip any coins," I warned.

"We won't," Mike said sympathetically. "We'll all go talk to her."

Karen nodded. "Let's go get her schedule, find out where she is."

Karen, Luke, and Mike were rushing out of the room faster than Groucho, Chico, and Harpo ever did. But Doug raised his hand and said, "Hold it, hold it, hold it."

They stopped in their tracks and turned around and looked at him. "Don't go now. Don't go yet."

"Why?"

"How come?"

"What do you mean?"

Doug waved them to sit down. "What are you going to do, barrel into one of her classes and tell her she's got to do it?"

"Doug's right," Karen agreed. "It's like what Ms. Naiman says whenever something big comes up—"

We were all nodding now, and said together,

" 'Let's give it a day to think what we want to do.' "

"Right," Luke agreed.

"Okay," Doug said. "We'll meet here after school today and decide the best plan of action. Then we'll all go to her homeroom before school tomorrow—we know she's always there early—and with no one else around, give her all the reasons we decided here after school why she should do it."

"I can't make it tonight," I told them. "My boss is leaving work, we're having a party, and I have to help set up."

"Okay, you're excused," Mike said with a grin. "But meet us here tomorrow at seven-thirty, and then we'll all go down to—Bill, what's her homeroom?"

"201."

"O-kayyyy!" Mike said, "and we'll go over to 201 and work on her."

They were all so sure of themselves, I didn't have the heart to tell them I had a feeling they were wasting their time.

And at that point I didn't even know the real bad part yet.

14

So, after school when I walked up Hemlock Street to get my car, it was like yesterday all over again. There was Mary leaning against it, waiting for me.

She must have changed her mind! She was going to be in the contest!

Someone driving by would have thought I was practicing for a hundred-yard dash. Come to think of it, someone driving by would have had trouble keeping up with me.

"Hi!" I said, managing to sound real warm even though I was out of breath.

But Mary only nodded a hi before saying, "I'm sorry about yesterday."

"That's all right," I said, meaning it—now that things, I was sure, were going to work out.

But she shook her head no and gave out the type of big sigh you give when the person you're talking to doesn't understand. "Can we go somewhere and talk?"

I'd already started unlocking her door when she got to the word "go." "Sure," I said, even though I had to get to the hotel and help with the party. I couldn't walk away from this, though.

All the way to the Sizzler I gave her a little

speech, saying stuff like I was hoping she'd decided not to quit, because the contest was a chance to let people hear about how some kids do nice things for others. "And maybe," I explained, "once people hear about everything you've done for Eddie, they might just get out and do something nice for somebody, too."

But all the while I was talking, Mary didn't say anything. She didn't even shake her head from side to side like she had yesterday. Whenever we stopped for a light and I'd look over, I'd see her just staring down at the floor. Yes, something else was going on here—but what?

So as I kept on telling her how wonderful she was, I was also thinking, once we get inside the restaurant, I'm going to let her do the talking . . .

Mary looked down away from me, and played with the straw in her iced coffee.

"The Isabella Stewart Gardner School for Girls, where I went before Dallin, has seventh, eighth, and ninth grades, not just seventh and eighth, like with most junior highs. After going there three years, I wanted to go to Linden High, right near my house, where all my best friends were going. For the last three years, they'd been at Linden Junior High without me, and that was long enough, as far as I was concerned.

"But," she said slowly, "Dad and Mom wanted me to go to another private school." She shrugged. "They kept saying, 'You can't compare the education you get at a public school with the great one you get at a private school,' all that stuff. I was just about to give in . . . until Jim came along. He went to Linden High, too."

She paused there, and played with the straw again. And though I didn't know what she could possibly be getting at, I thought maybe she needed me to help her over this tough part. "So when it ended with Jim, you decided to go to Dallin?"

She shook her head no. "I didn't want to go to Dallin because it'd take so long to get there."

"Sure," I agreed, remembering how long it took me to get out to her house.

"Ever done it by bus and subway?" she said with a scowl. "An hour and a half each way, sometimes more coming back, what with rush hour. I didn't even have my permit then, let alone my license. My father works way out in Salem, and my mother doesn't drive anymore."

She looked up then and saw I wanted to know why. "You probably noticed when you met Mom that she sits a little . . . stiffly. She's had some sort of equilibrium problem since Gina was born, so she doesn't have such really great control over her balance. Dad told me he never wanted to sell her car, sort of as a way to let her know he always had faith she'd get better."

She tossed the straw deep down into the drink and sat back and decided to look at me for a while. "But she never has. And with Mom still sick, I hated to have to argue with them about this Dallin/Linden High thing. And they hated it, too. Finally one night in July, they just got tired of fighting. They realized if I didn't want to go to Dallin, it'd really be stupid to force me." She shrugged again. "If I wasn't happy in school, maybe my marks'd drop, and then I'd really have trouble getting into college," she said, before crooking her fingers into quotation marks and adding, "The right college.

"Whatever the reason was, it was fine with me. Everything started going great then. It was right around the time I was turning sixteen—and starting drivers' ed to get my permit, which I got. And once I got it, I really didn't want to do anything but drive."

Though I still didn't know what Mary was getting at—and still had a feeling that I wasn't going to like it when she got to the point—I did have to smile, remembering what I felt a year and a half ago when I got my permit. "Sure," I agreed. "When I was a little kid and my parents'd say, 'Let's go for a ride,' I'd say, 'Ohhhhhh, just riding around's real boring. I hate going for rides where there's no destination.' But oh, when I got my permit, boy did I change my mind. I was dragging Mom out on rides I would've never gone on before."

The Mary I took out the other night would have laughed at that, but today's Mary just said a solemn "Right," and went on. "Anyway, everything was great until I found out Jim decided to fall in love with his friend's sister. After talking to everybody about it, I decided to talk to my father about it, too. I wanted to talk to him with no one else around, though, so I asked him if he'd take a ride with me, me driving, him being the adult in the car. We wound up at Eddie's."

She sat back and whooshed out a big breath. "Once we got inside the place, and Eddie told us how bad his eyes were getting, that's when I really felt so stupid. I'd been thinking Jim breaking up with me was the end of the whole world, and here was a guy who was starting to be afraid to drive early in the morning because the streetlights and the shadows made it hard for him. And the poor guy even found it worse at night! But what could he do? Like I said, it took two buses and a train to get to Ardmore . . ."

Her voice trailed off there. She didn't say anything else, but sat there, giving me all the time I'd need to figure it out. And finally thickheaded me figured it out.

"Oh . . ."

And she knew from my "Oh" that I'd gotten it. "That's right."

"Oh."

"Yes."

"When you're sixteen and have a permit—"

"That's right."

"—you can drive only as long as there's an adult in the car."

"Right."

"And you've got to be sixteen-and-a-half before you can drive all alone."

She was nodding slowly. "Yes. My parents didn't go for my plan right away. Dad felt it was breaking 'the spirit of the law,' because the adult in the car really should be able to see enough to drive. I argued that Eddie *could* see enough to drive, but just thought he'd better not. But by this time they knew I didn't want to go to Linden High where Jim was—well, you know, it must be tough for you if you ever run into April—"

"Yes."

"—and in the end they figured anything that got me to go to Dallin was worth it." Now she looked at me. "So," she breathed, "every day, Eddie walks over to my house in the morning. I drive him in—"

"—park in the parking lot behind his store—"

"—walk to Dallin, walk to the library after—"

"—walk to Eddie's after work—"

"—and drive him back to my house."

"And Eddie walks home," I said softly, finishing up the explanation.

She nodded again. "On the days my father isn't home yet to give him a ride." Now she looked right in my eyes. "But honest, Bill, it was never meant to be a secret. Eddie just never mentioned that part of it to you, I don't know why. Talking to him, why wouldn't you think I was Miss Inner Beauty? But it wasn't 'Inner Beauty' that made me do it. It was something like symbiosis in Biology . . . you know what I mean?"

I nodded slowly. "Something that helps both people."

"Yeah," she agreed. "Eddie would have a hard time getting to work without me, and I'd have a hard time getting to school without him."

The waitress came over and, unlike the one we'd had the last time, slowly and nicely put the check on the table, even giving us a smile and saying, "No rush." I looked at Mary, and she looked at me, then asked, "You think after this we can still be friends? Because," she added, "I know you went out with me just because you thought I was something terrific. And now that you see I'm not, I'd understand it if you never wanted to see me ever again."

What could I say, no? That I never really went out with her to be friends in the first place, but only because the kids wanted me to see if she could cut it for the contest? "Sure we can still be friends, of course we can still be friends."

"Well, then," she said, smiling, but, I could see, worried that this little joke wasn't going to work, "you mind driving me to the library?"

I smiled. "No."

She didn't. "No, meaning no-you-won't-drive-me or no, meaning no-you-don't-mind?"

"No, meaning no-I-don't-mind."

She looked down a second. "Thanks."

We left the place, got in the car, and didn't talk at all for the few minutes it took us to get to the library. I figured maybe it'd be a good idea for me to make some sort of joke, and I did the best I could.

"Well," I said as we pulled into the library parking lot, "at least you're really a volunteer two days a week at the library."

She made a *tsk* sound, then slowly shook her head no.

"You're not a volunteer? I thought you said—"

"No, yes, I volunteer. But you might as well know I don't just do it out of the goodness of my heart. One of the reasons I do it is to help me on the kids' book I'm writing."

"You're writing a kids' book?"

She nodded. *"The Antelope Who Loved Cantaloupe."*

"Ohhhhh," I said, remembering the title, "you wrote that?"

"Huh?" She looked at me really confused. "Why? You've heard of it? How? It isn't out yet—"

I let out a laugh through my nose. "That little kid the day I left you off, what's his name, Matthew—?"

She remembered and nodded. "Yes, Matthew! He's my biggest fan. What I do is write a chapter, then bring it in and read it to the kids. I keep in what keeps them in their chairs and rewrite the rest. Once I'm finished, I'm going to try and get it published, and, to be real honest with you, I hope it makes a lot of money. No, Bill, I'm not Miss Inner Beauty at all. If I'm anything, I'm just Miss Symbiosis."

Still, she put her hand on mine and squeezed it, more to comfort me, or to say, "I'm sorry I've hurt you." Her last line before she got out of the car and went up the library steps was, "I know now you just took me out because you thought I was something I'm not. And I'm sorry for that. But I am glad you still want to be my friend."

I felt the worst I'd felt since that night at *Give Her the Moon*. And I sure wasn't in the mood for Ms. Algarotti's surprise farewell party.

15

But everyone else was sure in the mood for a surprise farewell party. Luckily, Ms. Algarotti's office is downstairs right near the function rooms, so all we had to do was pull a fuse while she was sitting in there. Then, when she came out to see why all her lights had gone out—

"SURPRISE!!!"

Even though I was in a not-so-hot mood, I could see it was a great party. Ms. Algarotti's mother said the Italian food was as good as any she ever had or made. The band was great, playing songs you could hear on the radio, not old songs like the ones those ancient bands play at somebody's wedding. The gift we all chipped in to get her, Mary would be happy to know, sure wasn't a joke gift, but a VCR, plus videocassettes of three movies that were really fitting for a hotel manager: *Hotel*, *Grand Hotel*, and *Animal House*.

But after we gave her the gifts, I went back to my bad mood again. All my work friends had someone with them—Stan and Bob were with their wives, John was with his girlfriend, Rana with her boyfriend. . . and I had no one. Maybe I should have asked someone.

Maybe I should have asked Mary.

Right then I realized that if I'd brought her and introduced her as my girlfriend, everybody would have been happy for me, and wouldn't have worried that she wasn't April.

Of course, I tried to look around and see if there was anybody I liked who I might want to get to know. Funny: There was that new waitress I thought was kind of pretty . . . though I didn't know why. She wasn't my usual type—no long-straw-hair going down to her waist—but there was something about her . . .

By the end of the night, though, I did decide on one thing: If I ever wanted to know for sure whether or not April got the job for me when Ms. Algarotti saw us at the mall, tonight would have to be the night. And I did want to know. After all, how important is it to the world that you have a terrific-looking girl on your arm?

So by one in the morning when everything was pretty much winding down, when we were all huddled around Ms. A. to say our last good-byes, I got at the very end of the line. After everybody else had finished and left the place, I'd ask her then.

When I reached her, though, I didn't have the nerve to get to the big question right away. Instead I told her to look up my father when she got to New York, and gave her his business card. Ms. Algarotti raised it the way you toast with a glass of champagne and let me know she just might do it.

Then she put out her hand for me to shake. I took it and gave it a good pump. Trouble was, I could feel from her handshake that she was tired and wouldn't be in the mood to talk, especially about something heavy. I just took my hand away and almost took a step to leave.

But no, I decided. This was my last chance! And I had to know. "Ms. Algarotti?"

"Yes, Bill?"

"I need to know something."

"Oh?"

"I need to know why you hired me."

I could tell she was real surprised I asked. "Why I hired you?"

"Yeah," I said. "What exactly was it about me that made you hire me instead of someone else? Can you remember?"

She made a little face that told me she was trying to remember the day it happened. "Well, I remember I liked your attitude," she said, in a way that made it sound like she could have given a hundred other reasons. "I remember you didn't just answer my questions with a 'yes' or 'no,' but you actually talked. That gave me the impression that you liked talking, and if there's one thing we need in a hotel to make a guest feel like he's at home, it's someone who likes to talk." Then, instead of going on with a few more reasons, she looked at me with a squint and wanted to know, "Why are you asking?"

"Oh . . ." I said, putting my hands in my pockets, getting a little embarrassed now. "I was just wondering . . ."

She saw there was still something I wasn't telling her. "Wondering what?" she continued.

Okay, I'd come right out and ask her. "Did it have anything to do with April?"

"*April*?"

From the way she said it, I knew what the answer was. Still, I had to explain. "Remember the next day after the interview you ran into me at the mall and I was with April?"

She squinted and tried to remember. "Really? Is that what happened?"

"Yeah," I said, pretty surprised she didn't remember. Was she really telling me the truth? "Yeah, it seemed like you were looking at me in a way that said you admired me."

"Well," she agreed, "I probably was."

Now I was even ashamed to say it, but I had to be without-a-doubt sure. "But I thought it might have been because you saw me with such a beautiful girl. I mean, if I could get her, then I must be—"

She wouldn't even let me finish, because she wanted me to know how stupid the whole thing was. "Bill! You mean you don't know that you got the job just because of yourself?"

"W-well," I stuttered, "I just thought . . . well, at the interview, you didn't tell me right away I got the job, and then the next day when y—"

"Bill," she said, cocking her head at an angle, "most employers don't tell an applicant on the spot whether or not he got the job. Most want to think about it a day or two."

Funny, I thought, I should have realized that from what Ms. Naiman had always told us—"Let's give it a day to think what we want to do."

I guess love at first sight doesn't mean much on job interviews, either, I decided as I left the place. Alone.

Alone. All because I didn't want to ask Mary. Because I didn't want to be kidded by the guys that I was ready to take a chance with a girlfriend. Because I thought having a girl with outer beauty was more important than one with inner beauty.

Was I stupid or what?

16

The next morning, when I put my hand on the office doorknob, I could hear the kids' voices from behind the door. That made me take my hand off right away again.

No. I had to go in.

I opened the door real slowly, figuring that'd at least let them know I wasn't optimistic about our chances for convincing Mary.

All four of them were sitting and counting votes. "Okay," Mike said. "Mary's got 77 votes, Fifer's got 51, Sobolow 44, and Ronan 19. When you consider our circulation's 194—"

"193," I said dully. "Don't forget Rick Kravitz canceled."

"When you consider our circulation's 193," Mike said in the same tone as before—letting me know he wasn't in the mood for jokes, "you can see that it's mathematically impossible for your girl to lose."

"It's like," Luke helped out, "a team that's got a thirteen-game lead with twelve games left in the season."

"So," Karen said, "here's our plan to convince her to stay in the cont—"

She stopped because she saw me shaking my head no. "We got a disaster on our hands that makes the Texas Chain Saw Massacre look like a birthday party at McDonald's. . . ."

They were furious while I first told them, but after I finished telling them everything, they were pretty quiet.

Finally I thought I'd better say something. After all, I was the one who'd started all this. "So," I concluded, "what do you want to do?"

Karen took her finger away from her mouth. "I guess we'd better check with Ms. Naiman and see what she thinks."

"I hate calling her any more than we have to," Mike said. "And we got ourselves into this, so we should really get ourselves out."

"There's something else I'm thinking of," said Doug. "We're newspapermen. The public has a right to know." He stuck out his jaw. "We should really be printing the truth, and . . ."

Doug's the type of guy who doesn't finish his sentences until he's sure everyone's going to agree with him. But I knew what he was thinking, so I'd finish it for him: "Expose Mary for the fraud that she is?"

"Well," he mumbled.

Now I was mad. "Let's just electrocute her."

And now he was mad. "Why don't we?"

Luke made a face. "We should electrocute the guy who makes the doughnuts for not telling us the whole story."

Well, I heard a lot of "You bets" and "Rights!" over that one. And even though Eddie is my friend, I was pretty mad at him for not telling me everything.

* * *

"Ed, why didn't you tell me the whole story?"

He didn't look like Santa Claus now, but like a little kid who's been caught telling a lie. "Gee, Bill, I'm really sorry. I just brought her up so you'd get to know her. You were so miserable over April, she was ready to throw herself off a bridge over that Jim jerk . . ."

"Yeah, but look what happened."

His eyes widened and he extended his hands in front of him. "Bill, did I know you were going to start giving out trophies? I just thought I'd fix up two nice kids I know. I figured if you heard how good a kid she was, you might ask her out to a dance or something."

"Yeah, but—"

He didn't want any buts. "And anyway, you were right when you nominated her for your contest thing. Sure she drove me in because she needed an adult in the car with her. But that's not what she's been doing the last two months."

"What do you mean, the last two months?"

"She's sixteen-and-a-half now. Has been for two months. She's got her license."

"What?"

"Yeah, she's old enough to drive by herself now. She doesn't take me in anymore because she has to." He looked me in the eye to make it official. "She does it because she wants to."

I gulped down the last of my coffee. "Excuse me, Ed—I've got to run."

"Hey, don't you want to finish your honeydip?"

"*No.*"

I sure didn't. Instead I got in my car and sped over to the library, zipped up the stairs at the kiddie wing, and barged in. I didn't know where I was going, but I'd decided to just walk down the long hall with rooms on each side until I heard Mary's voice coming from one of them. And I finally did:

". . . 'I'd like to run away and get married,' said the Antelope, 'but I can't elope without my cantaloupe.' "

I rushed into the room her voice was coming from. There she was—in the middle of a group of kids, so into what she was doing that she didn't even notice me come in.

One little kid did, though. "Mister, you want to hear about the Antelope Who Loved Cantaloupe?!"

That got Mary to look up. "Bill!"

"That your boyfriend, Mary?" asked one little girl.

"Mary," I asked, "can I talk to you alone?"

"He *is* Mary's boyfriend!" squealed the little girl.

Mary got as red as Eddie's shirt, but she came over to the doorway to meet me. That wasn't good enough—I pulled her outside away from her kids. "How old are you?"

"How old am I?"

"Yes, how old are you?"

She blinked. "Sixteen."

"Oh, yeah? When's your birthday?"

"July third."

"Then you're sixteen-and-a-half."

"Well, yeah, but who counts halves after you're ten?"

"*I* do! Because it means now you *don't* need Eddie every day!"

A little boy ran out of the room. "Mary, I thought we had to be quiet in the library—"

"Yes, Jason, that's right." She turned back and looked at me with a smile. "But not everybody knows it."

"Mister," the kid said, wagging a finger, "you hafta be quiet—"

"That's all right, Jason, I'll tell him. Now go inside, I'll be right back in—"

"You're sixteen-and-a-half," I said again, not caring that I was loud or that four-year-olds were taking all of this in. "You're sixteen-and-a-half and you're still getting up at five-thirty to drive him in!"

She lifted up her arms and flapped them against her side in frustration. "Come on, Bill, what was I going to do once I didn't need him anymore—make him close up the shop?"

"And you weren't going to tell me?!"

Another exhausted breath. "There've been so many hassles over this I didn't want to."

"Shhhhhhhhhhhh!" said one nosy little boy who popped out of the room. Then he laughed his head off.

"Get inside," I hissed, "or you're not going to live to be five!"

"Bill! I'm surprised at you! How can you—"

"Later we'll talk about how I scare kids! Right now I just want to know if you're still going to take Eddie in the rest of the year!"

She made an exasperated face. "Yes! Of course! And next year, if he wants, and the year after that, too."

"I knew it!" I yelled. "You're Miss Inner Beauty after all! Come on! Be in the contest!"

For a second, she didn't say anything. And just as I was ready to go into a real long plea, giving her every reason on earth why I thought she deserved it, she shook her head yes, just a little, but yes.

That's when I kissed her. Which is when all the nosy little kids popped their heads out of the room and watched these two grown-ups kissing.

"Oooooooooooooooooooooooooooooooooooh!" they said.

I stopped kissing Mary for a second, looked at them, and pointed. "Some day you'll understand!" I said. Mary laughed, and I did, too, until I grabbed her and kissed her again and again and again.

DALLINEWS

The Newspaper of Dallin High School
Ardmore, Massachusetts

EXTRA!

NEW MISS INNER BEAUTY CONTEST INFORMATION!

An Open Letter from "Name Withheld":

Blame everything on me. It was my mistake.

No wonder I'm still going to sign this "Name Withheld."

Journalists always say that the public has a right to know. So I want to tell you that Mary Mulcahy has *not*, repeat *NOT*, been getting up at 5:30 in the morning and driving Eddie Petrucci to and from work every day since school began just to help him.

Seems that Mary drove Eddie to work every day because she only had a permit and needed an adult to drive in with her. As Mary explains it, "It was symbiosis." She got to drive to Dallin instead of taking the T, and Eddie got to keep his doughnut shop open.

However, in the last two months—before, I might add, the whole idea for the Miss Inner Beauty Contest started—Mary's gotten her license and doesn't need that adult in the car anymore. Still, she's getting up at 5:30 and taking Eddie to work each day—and plans to keep doing it.

As I said, the public has a right to know—so I want you to know that Mary Mulcahy's doing it now not because she has to, but because she wants to.

Still, this new information may make you want to change your vote. And if you do, *Dallinews* says you can. Inside you'll find a new ballot for a new Miss Inner Beauty election.

Dallinews regrets the error. But we also understand symbiosis. After all, we're glad to give whoever's voted Miss Inner Beauty the opportunity to be recognized, while *we* get national recognition from *USA Today* and broadcast coverage from *Local Focals*. Everybody wins! Maybe the moral of this whole story is that if more people did things to help other people, they'd find that they'd be helping themselves at the same time. And what's wrong with that?

17

What a night! Mayor Kinsman shook my hand. And Ms. Naiman, making a triumphant return appearance, looked just terrific. Staying out of school all that time obviously agreed with her.

It was great seeing all the big trucks with the Channel 4/Group W symbols on them out in front of the school. They had cables the size of sewer pipes snaking around from them, going all across the parking lot and into O'Gorman Hall. What seemed like a hundred guys were running around with lights and poles, and lightpoles too. Funny how they looked bored—we sure weren't.

Gerri Jontry was a great hostess with all four M.I.B. finalists—including Mary. Each one of the girls had camera presence like you wouldn't believe—including Mary.

It was while I was looking at Mary, though, that I realized something: the waitress whose looks I liked at Ms. Algarotti's party? I hadn't put two and two together back then, but now I did: the reason I liked her looks was because she looked a little like Mary. Somehow I was changing my type.

"And Miss Inner Beauty is," cried Ms. Jontry, opening the envelope, ". . . Miss Mary Mulcahy!"

As the crowd cheered, Mary strolled right up to the podium, took her roses, and bent her head ever-so-slightly so that her attendants could put the crown on her head. And damn if she didn't go right into her Future-Anchorwoman-in-Providence act. She smiled at the cameras, waved at everybody, and held her bouquet of roses like a pro. She even waited for everyone to stop applauding and cheering before she started to speak:

"Thank you very much. There is one thing that's bothering me, though. I don't see why this had to be only a *Miss* Inner Beauty Contest. Sure, there's Miss America and Miss Universe, but there's also a *Mr.* America and *Mr.* Universe, too. So shouldn't we also have a *Mr.* Inner Beauty?

"I have a nominee," she said, "for this year's Mr.—Inner Handsomeness?" The audience laughed. "He's the guy who came up with the idea of the Miss Inner Beauty Contest to begin with—and I think that anyone who wants to have a contest to make a big deal out of Inner Beauty must have a lot of Inner Handsomeness himself, right?"

"Right!" a few people yelled, as I thought about leaving the hall. But, no, I wouldn't. Mary had started this, she wanted me up there, and I couldn't embarrass her by refusing to go up. But as she went on, I thought about the day April cornered me in front of the office and called me Mr. Inner Beauty in a sarcastic way. I liked what was happening now better:

"When I was thinking of dropping out of the contest," Mary went on, "one person kept saying to me, 'Don't! The contest is a chance to let people hear about how some people do nice things for other people. And maybe once they hear about everything you've done, they might just get out and do something nice for somebody, too.' Is that Inner Handsomeness? I think so. Ladies and gentlemen, may I introduce—Bill Richards!"

As I walked up to the stage, as everyone cheered, as Mike, Luke, Doug, Karen, everybody was patting me on the back, I wondered what I was going to do when I got up there. I mean, I'm a reporter, not a performer. We journalists usually stay behind the scenes.

But all I did was give Mary a big kiss in front of the whole school. That way, there wouldn't just be rumors about us going all around Dallin—there'd be facts.

Afterwards, after the last camera crew left and all that remained were a hundred thousand shreds of crepe paper, Mary and I walked to the parking lot.

"Hungry?" I asked.

"Starving."

"Let's go somewhere."

"We can take my car," she said.

"I know. You've got your license."

And as we walked hand in hand to her '74 Mustang, she asked, "I hope I didn't embarrass you too much by calling you up there."

"Not *too* much."

She let go of my hand to make a gesture. "I tried to keep it short and simple. I had hundreds of things to say, but I thought you might be too embarrassed if I made you stand there while I kept saying great things about you. But," she added, "would you like to hear what I didn't say?"

Like everybody, I don't mind hearing good things said about me. "Sure!"

She laughed, because she knew I was into it. "Bill's great fun on a date," she started, counting off on her fingers. "He knows sports. If you're upset, he'll talk to you. If you ask him out he doesn't take advantage but is polite enough to ask you out in return—"

That's when I had to start laughing, but Mary just kept on going: "He tries to calm you down when you're upset and doesn't think you're an idiot for crying, and lets you explain as much as you want, or none at all if you don't—"

That's when I had to kiss her. I put my two arms around her waist, pulled her close to me.

She kept talking even through the kiss "When you tell him to jiggle the key, he doesn't tell you to mind your own business, but just jiggles."

Kiss!

"He can tell you some funny hotel stories—"

Kiss!

"He offers you some of his strawberry shortcake after you say you don't want any, and doesn't mind when you take some after all—"

Kiss! Kiss!

"—and, last but not least, he says that Mrs. Weingarten is heavyset instead of calling her Beachball!"

Now that she was finished, she threw her arms around my neck and gave me a phenomenal kiss back. Then came one long, long, lovely, wonderful one.

"I love you, Mary."

"I love you, Bill."

"I know," I joked. "You just made that kinda clear."

"But I'm still starving."

"Me *too,*" I said.

''Want to dig into my twenty-five-pound box of candy?''

''No,'' I laughed. ''Let's go to the Captain of the Guard.''

''The Captain of the Guard?''

''It's the restaurant at the hotel where I work. It's really nice there. And you can meet all my friends. . .''